Photo: Gudren Likar

STEPHEN SEWELL is one of Australia's most experienced and prominent writers, and his writing has won many awards. As a playwright, he is well-known for his violently political dramas such as *Traitors*, *Welcome the Bright World* and *The Blind Giant is Dancing*. Other playwriting credits include *The Father We Loved on a Beach by the Sea*, *Dust*, *The Garden of Granddaughters*, *The Sick Room*, *The Secret Death of Salvador Dali* and *Three Furies: Scenes from the Life of Francis Bacon*. His screenwriting credits include *The Boys* (winner of 1998 AFI for Best Screenplay adapted from another source), *Sisters* and *Lost Things*. *Myth, Propaganda and Disaster in Nazi Germany and Contemporary America—A Drama in 30 Scenes* was first produced by Playbox in association with the State Theatre Company of South Australia in 2003. It has had much-lauded productions overseas, including London and Germany, and in 2005 it will play in Edinburgh and New York. It has won more awards than any Australian play in history.

D1518309

MYTH, PROPAGANDA AND DISASTER IN NAZI GERMANY AND CONTEMPORARY AMERICA

A DRAMA IN 30 SCENES

STEPHEN SEWELL

Currency Press · Sydney

CURRENCY PLAYS

First published in 2003
by Currency Press Pty Ltd,
PO Box 2287, Strawberry Hills, NSW, 2012, Australia
enquiries@currency.com.au
www.currency.com.au

This revised edition published 2005

Copyright © Stephen Sewell, 2003, 2005

NATIONAL LIBRARY OF AUSTRALIA CIP DATA
    Sewell, Stephen, 1953–.
        Myth, propaganda and disaster in Nazi Germany and contemporary
        America: a drama in 30 scenes.
        Rev. ed.
        ISBN 0 86819 775 0.
        I. Title. (Series: Currency plays).
    A822.3

Set by Dean Nottle
Cover design by Mollison
Printed by Southwood Press, Marrickville, NSW

Contents

'Know reality for what it is.'
Marcus Aurelius

Introduction

Stephen Sewell

The assault on international law and democratic institutions currently being waged under the guise of the War on Terror has provoked a storm of protest throughout the world, and within the theatre community, and *Myth, Propaganda and Disaster in Nazi Germany and Contemporary America—A Drama in 30 Scenes* is part of that reaction. With its roots in the great tradition of humanist opposition to absurdity and tyranny, from Kafka's *The Trial* through to Arthur Miller's *The Crucible* and Brecht's *Galileo*, *Myth* tells the story of Talbot Finch—a name chosen to evoke America's own great liberal tradition, in the name of Atticus Finch, the hero of *To Kill a Mockingbird*—as he suffers a mysterious persecution at the hands of someone only he can see, and whose existence is denied by all around him. Caught in this nightmarish trap, Talbot questions his own sanity as he confronts the question each of us is asking at the moment: is this really happening and what can I do to protect myself? What can I do to protect myself from a State that can dispense with any pretence to legal obligations and practices simply by calling me a terrorist? What can I do to protect myself when the ancient prohibitions against torture are being flouted in a gulag of secret prisons dotted across the globe, filled with ghost prisoners apparently beyond the reach of even the International Red Cross and the Geneva Conventions? How can I protect myself when my own Government is complicit in the kidnapping and torture of Australian citizens and happy to lie on a daily basis about its knowledge and involvement in international crime? How can I protect myself now?

The answer is now well known. On my own, it is impossible to protect myself in all but the most rudimentary of ways, but as a group we can protect ourselves from the tyrants who are ever ready to take away our lives and rights. This is not empty rhetoric, this is the core element of democracy: for good or for evil, the power of the group is infinitely greater than the power of the individual. This is a truth that has been proven again and again, both in the positive and the negative senses. The Nazis won in Germany because they were able to corral and annihilate any opposition, and herd the many German people they had not murdered into the Nazi Party itself. In the famous words of Pastor Martin Niemöller, 'In Germany they first came for the Communists, and I didn't speak up because I wasn't a Communist. Then they came for the Jews, and I didn't speak up because I wasn't a Jew. Then they came for the trade unionists, and I didn't speak up because I wasn't a trade unionist. Then they came for the Catholics, and I didn't speak up because I was a Protestant. Then they came for me—and by that time no one was left to speak up.'

On a more positive note, the ability of people to confront and defeat the bullies and little Hitlers in our midst is a daily experience, and one that should encourage us to take heart in the community we are a part of. And part of the expression of that community is theatre.

Theatre has nearly always been on the side of the oppressed and the vulnerable because theatre, even in its most ancient forms, has used as its material human lives and dilemmas, and presented these in a communal setting. Of all the arts, theatre is most unique in its direct relationship with its audience. Theatre is the people speaking to themselves, and in speaking to themselves, creating a sense of their own unity. This is why autocrats from Plato down have been suspicious or downright condemnatory of the theatrical arts, and this is why politics and theatre have always had such an intimate relationship. The Velvet Revolution that overthrew Communism in the former Czechoslovakia was forged in Vaclav Havel's Magic Theatre in Prague, where the Oppositionists met and plotted the downfall of the old regime, and this is but one of the most recent links in the long chain that has found theatre and political action synonymous. Theatre is politics and politics is theatre, and so long as the rulers control the other forms of mass media, theatre will remain the avenue through which we can inform one another of how we really feel.

And how we feel now is angry, frightened and confused. How we feel now is bewildered as the world we have known of laws and rights and democracy are stripped away and replaced by an Ancient Regime of arbitrary power we thought died centuries ago. But we should not be disheartened. We know that while tyranny presents itself as strong, it is fundamentally weak, relying as it does on the absolute power of an individual, and what makes it weak is what makes us strong, and we will win this fight against those who would lock us up and torture us because we are humanity willing itself to thrive and live. We know their lies for what they are, and know their most corrosive lie—'you are alone'—is the biggest lie of all, because we know we are not alone, and when we sit in a theatre hearing each other breathe as the joys and fears of our lives are presented onstage, we know the truth: we are not alone, and we are not afraid.

Sydney
June 2005

'Naturally the common people don't want war, but after all, it is the leaders of a country who determine the policy, and it is always a simple matter to drag people along whether it is a democracy, or a fascist dictatorship, or a parliament, or a communist dictatorship. Voice or no voice, the people can always be brought to the bidding of the leaders. This is easy. All you have to do is to tell them they are being attacked, and denounce the pacifists for lack of patriotism and exposing the country to danger. It works the same in every country.'

Hermann Goering,
Hitler's Reich-Marshall
at the Nuremberg Trials
after World War II.

Myth, Propaganda and Disaster in Nazi Germany and Contemporary America was first produced by Playbox Theatre, in collaboration with the State Theatre Company of South Australia, at The C.U.B. Malthouse, Melbourne, on 4 June 2003, with the following cast:

TALBOT	Nicholas Eadie
EVE	Alison Whyte
MARGURITE	Ming-Zhu Hii
JACK	Michael Habib
AMY	Jacqy Phillips
STAN	Robert Macpherson
JILL	Martha Lott
MAX	Tom Considine
MAN	Greg Stone

Director, Aubrey Mellor
Designer, Shaun Gurton
Lighting Designer, Mark Shelton
Sound Design, David Franzke

CHARACTERS

TALBOT
EVE
MARGURITE
JACK
AMY
STAN
JILL
MAX
MAN
SECURITY GUARD
THERAPIST
STUDENTS, GUARDS

ACT ONE

SCENE ONE

University lecture hall.

An American-sounding man in his forties is addressing a collection of students as slides illustrating his talk flash through the dark space, occasionally lighting the large American flag hanging from the ceiling.

TALBOT: ... So that what you really have, for all their claims to rationality—And what you must remember is the incredible organisational skill that went into keeping the trains running on time, and the ovens stoked, even as the Reich itself was being devoured by the victorious invading armies—for all their quite justified claims to running an efficient and rationally organised killing machine, the facts of the matter are that these very clear thinking men—Eichmann, Speer, Himmler and the rest—were involved in a deeply irrational struggle they were bound to undertake given the mythic hobgoblins unleashed in their psyche by Nazism, and prominently displayed in Nazi propaganda, in order to justify itself. For if the racial purity of the superior Aryan was the supreme value, then the Nazi supermen had no choice but to exterminate the Jews or become degenerate and be exterminated in their turn, and when it became clear to Hitler in those last lonely days of *Gotterdamerung* in his Berlin bunker that Aryan Germany had indeed lost the struggle, he actively embraced extermination and death by ordering Speer to destroy Germany's remaining food and fuel supplies so that the nation would starve and freeze to death rather than linger on as a degenerate slave race under the boots of the despised Slavs. In the end, the madness that had only been implicit at the outset, and that no one believed anyone in their right mind could possibly mean, consumed everything, and the rational was revealed as nothing more than the hand-maiden of the completely insane.

The last image is of a little Jewish boy holding his hands up in surrender as a Nazi soldier points his gun at him.

FIRST VOICE: [*voice-over*] Then what's the point?

TALBOT: Point?

FIRST VOICE: [*voice-over*] Of thinking; of trying to work things out?

SECOND VOICE: [*voice-over*] If all we're doing when we try to think rationally is working out clever ways of committing insane acts, what's the point of thinking?

TALBOT: I believe you have just stumbled onto one of the saddest riddles of Western thought.

FIRST VOICE: [*voice-over*] I'm serious, Professor: what's the point of thinking?

TALBOT *is bringing things to a close.*

TALBOT: The hope that one day we might find the truth, and as someone famous once said—it was either Mulder or Jesus—'The truth might set us free'.

But another voice calls through the darkness.

MAN: [*voice-over*] I have a question, Professor...

There is something odd and commanding about the voice that makes TALBOT *peer out into the shadows.*

TALBOT: Yes...?

MAN: [*voice-over*] If all nations, as you say, are ultimately undone by the myths that found them, what will be the fate of America?

TALBOT: America, sir?

MAN: [*voice-over*] Yes. America.

TALBOT: What do you think?

MAN: [*voice-over*] No. What do you think?

TALBOT *picks up his briefcase and collects his papers.*

TALBOT: I think it's already happened.

MAN: [*voice-over*] What?

TALBOT: I think America has entered the kingdom of Fantasyland.

Chortle-chortle, ha-ha...

The lights change as TALBOT *moves off and for a moment we see the swastika illuminated on the stars and stripes, before a voice calls out...*

MARGURITE: Professor…

> *It's a pretty Asian girl running up.*

> Professor…?

TALBOT: Yes?

MARGURITE: I wonder if I could see you—I'm having trouble with one of the essay questions.

> TALBOT *makes a move.*

TALBOT: Talk to your tutor.

MARGURITE: I did, but he said I should talk to you—It's the Political Statics question—

TALBOT: I'm sorry…

MARGURITE: Margurite—Margurite Lee.

TALBOT: I'm sorry, Miss Lee, we've got a lock-down drill in five minutes—I really can't talk.

MARGURITE: Can I see you in your rooms?

> TALBOT *takes off.*

TALBOT: Make an appointment with the Faculty Secretary.

MARGURITE: I really enjoy your lectures, Professor!

TALBOT: Got to go.

MARGURITE: 'Bye!

> *Just then, an ominous-sounding alarm begins as a voice comes over the loudspeakers.*

SECURITY: [*voice-over*] Would all staff and students go immediately to their muster points. This is a lock-down. Would all staff and students proceed immediately to their muster points.

> *Light change.*

◆ ◆ ◆ ◆ ◆

SCENE TWO

Talbot's home.

A beautiful, sophisticated woman in a black dress is preparing a salad in the kitchen as TALBOT *pours himself a drink.*

EVE: … So eventually the right part arrived and he took it out and that's when he discovered that all it was was one of those plastic-bottlecap-type things—those flanges inside the bottle top—stuck in the outflow—It was a waste of the entire morning—We didn't need to replace the motor at all.

TALBOT: The pleasure's of consumerism...

EVE: And I've got a deadline—Will you set the VCR? My episode of *CSI* is on tonight.

TALBOT: What happens in this one? Plato decides the real is an illusion and has Socrates poisoned?

EVE: No, that was last week—What happens is the decomposed body of a teenage hooker—

TALBOT: I'll set the VCR.

EVE: Hey, I'm the one pulling the moolah around here—You know how much they're paying me for *West Wing*?

TALBOT: Go on, frighten me.

EVE: Oh, by the way, your publisher rang.

TALBOT: My publisher? When?

EVE: He asked you to call—I think he thinks the book's a little academic and wants a few more sex scenes.

TALBOT: Don't we all.

EVE: Hey, I'm wearing my Yves Saint Laurent underwear, if you really want to know.

TALBOT: Well, that must have really thrilled the plumber.

EVE: Yeah, he could barely keep his hands off the knobs.

TALBOT: So when did the publisher ring?

EVE: Just before you got home—And this guy tonight, he's your boss, right?

TALBOT: My boss, yeah.

EVE: And the other one...?

TALBOT: Is the Faculty lawyer.

EVE: So we're talking serious brown-nosing here—Who's who?

TALBOT: Jack's the Head of the Department and Stan's the lawyer.

EVE: And what's in it for me?

TALBOT: You just wait, baby; if they confirm my tenure, it'll be neapolitan ice cream from here on in.

EVE: You really know the way to a girl's heart—So what time are they arriving?

TALBOT: Eight—What's the time now? I might just have a shower...

TALBOT *begins to move off.*

EVE: It's just a marinara and salad—is that all right? I got some crusty bread.

TALBOT: Are you ready?

He disappears and the sound of the shower is heard as EVE *continues.*

EVE: Ready? Yes; yes, I'm ready, Talbot—Ready for what, I don't know—I was working on this scene today—you know, in the movie— where the mother discovers that the little girl is gone and I was just—struck—by how awful that must be—how terrible—It must be the worst thing in the world to lose a child—In fact, I can't imagine how you'd ever recover—I suddenly felt a terrible, terrible emptiness—a cold emptiness inside—Do you think that, really, that is our purpose in this world? To care for children? To bring them into being and watch them grow? If it is, then I wonder what on earth I'm doing. Why am I living the life I'm living—parties, forums, international blahdy-blahs?—Listen to me prattle—What's that? The *ennui*—Yes, *ennui*, of the proper bourgeois wife—'Moscow, Moscow—we must work'—when maybe it's all terribly simple after all, and all I have to do is forget my contraceptive pill one night—But as you say, Talbot, if we had children, we'd no longer have each other, would we?—We'd just start turning into things to one another— Sometimes I think I'm turning into a thing even now—Why is that, Talbot? Why is it that just when you think you've solved it, you realise you haven't even started?

'Ding-dong'... the front door chimes, and TALBOT *greets...*

TALBOT: Jack—Amy... Come in.

JACK *and* AMY *enter, taking the place in.*

I hope you didn't have any trouble with Security—

JACK: Security? No—Wow, look at this...

AMY: It's beautiful...

JACK: It's beautiful, Talbot—We must be paying you more than I thought!

AMY: It's beautiful, Talbot.

'Ding-dong'... and TALBOT'*s off again.*

JACK: Manhattan, ay—look at that...

EVE *steps out.*

EVE: [*greeting*] Hi, I'm Eve—I'm Talbot's—

JACK: Eve—I'm so pleased to meet you—We've both heard so much about you.

AMY: You're a novelist...?

EVE: Television writer.

JACK: Television...

TALBOT *returns with* STAN...

TALBOT: It's Stan!

JACK: Stan!

... *and his wife* JILL.

AMY: Hi, Jill...

JILL: Long time, no...

AMY: Yeah...

JILL: [*explaining*] We saw each other at FAO Schwartz this morning— There was another security scare down there—can you believe that? People had their own gas masks, for God's sake...

TALBOT: What can I get you guys to drink? Campari?

AMY: I'll have a campari.

JACK: I'll have mine with a little ice—Were you here on nine-eleven?

TALBOT: Yes...

JILL: Gee, you would have been able to see everything...

The guests are now lounging at a long table, philosophising at the end of an enjoyable meal. Another man, MAX, *has joined the table.*

JACK: ... Well, I know you've got a bee in your bonnet about it, Talbot, and it's certainly an interesting idea, but you can't take this myth thing too far, can you?

STAN: What do you actually mean by it, Talbot?

TALBOT: It's really pretty simple, Stan: you're a lawyer, right?

His wife, JILL, *horse-laughs.*

JILL: So-called.

TALBOT: So part of your education would have involved learning the myths of the law.

STAN: Such as...?

TALBOT: Well, that the law is blind—

STAN: That's not a myth—It might not always be true, but it's not a myth.

TALBOT: It is a myth. African Americans make up thirteen percent of the population, but forty-nine percent of the prison population—If the law's blind why is there such a disproportionate number of blacks in prison?

STAN: Well, there could be lots of reasons—

JACK: Come on, let's stick to the point.

TALBOT: My point is that every nation is constituted by a set of myths about who we are and where we're going, and those myths can blind us from the reality of what we're doing and impel us toward our own destruction.

STAN: So what's the American myth?

TALBOT: The myth of our own righteousness.

JILL: You're saying we deserve it?

TALBOT: What?

JILL: You're saying we deserve it? Those pricks flying their planes—

AMY: Our planes.

JILL: Into our buildings—We deserve it?

TALBOT: No—

JILL: I don't feel like I'm some sleep-walker stumbling around the place—

TALBOT: That's not what I said—

JILL: Well, what else—?

STAN: What did you say? Countries aren't abstract things, they're collections of people; people like us—If countries are constituted by myths, then we're the ones who believe them. What do you think is mythical about our beliefs?

JILL: We should have worn our cowboy hats, Stan.

TALBOT: You're both making it very personal.

JILL: It is personal. I had a friend in the North Tower. One of my best friends died in the North Tower. It is personal.

TALBOT: The CIA is torturing people to death—

JILL: That's a lie; that's a filthy lie.

TALBOT: The CIA is torturing people to death with the full knowledge—

JILL: Tell him, Stan; tell him it's a lie.

STAN: [to JILL] Just listen, sweetheart.

TALBOT: [*completing his sentence*] —with the full knowledge of the President and the Secretary of Defense—not just with their knowledge, with their encouragement—we are torturing people to death, sitting here in New York watching re-runs of *Seinfeld*, and imagining ourselves to be the guardians of freedom and democracy in the world. That is the kind of delusional myth that is endangering democracy in this country.

STAN: Well, that's quite a mouthful. Where would you like me to start in telling you you're wrong?

JILL: I'll tell him myself: minor abuse by inexperienced and frightened reservists—

AMY: I'm glad they're being tortured.

JACK: Oh, no, Amy...

AMY: I'm glad they're being tortured, and I hope that as they're being tortured, they think of every single one of those two thousand, eight hundred and nineteen people they sent plummeting to their deaths; I hope they think of all the hundreds of people they've sent to their deaths since—

JILL: They're blowing up child care centres, for God's sake! They're leaving bombs in litter bins!

AMY: And I can tell you, if I was there now, I'd buy my popcorn and I'd line up to pay my ten dollars to watch.

TALBOT: America is under attack...

JACK: Look, Talbot, obviously this is a sensitive issue, so maybe we should—

TALBOT: Do you believe in democracy, Amy? Do you believe in the rule of law?

AMY: Yes, I do; but you don't, do you?

TALBOT: Yes, I do.

AMY: No, you don't; you don't believe in democracy; you think we're all deluded; you think we imagine ourselves to be the guardians of freedom and democracy, as you said, when really we're fascists torturing people to death in dark, rat-infested cells—That's what you believe, isn't it?

JILL: I hope they do kill them. I hope they get every single one of those filthy terrorists, and I hope they kill them.

AMY: Is that what you think, Talbot?

TALBOT: I think that this is a dangerous time when everyone has to be very careful about what they do and say, because if we're not careful, we're going to bring the world down on top of us.

JACK turns to the last man, who has remained silent throughout this conversation.

JACK: What about you, Max? You haven't said anything yet. What do you think about the way we're handing things.

As soon as he opens his mouth, we know that MAX *is an Australian.*

MAX: I think you're great. You guys are just great.

Light change.

◆ ◆ ◆ ◆ ◆

SCENE THREE

Refectory.

A slide projects the slogan 'Land of the Free' onto the wall as the hollow sound of plates and cutlery rise around us and TALBOT *and* MAX *make their way toward a table carrying trays of refectory food.*

MAX: I couldn't believe last night.

TALBOT: I know! And they're the intellectuals! That's the intelligentsia, Max.

MAX: Not them, you—Are you out of your mind?

TALBOT: What?

MAX: All that crap you were going on about: 'We are torturing people to death, sitting here in New York watching *Seinfeld'*—What are you going on about, mate? You've got it made.

TALBOT: Hey, I didn't ask to have a fight about torture—Torture, for fuck's sake—Did you in your wildest dreams ever imagine you'd need to defend your opposition to torture to another civilized human being?

MAX: What are you talking about, Talbot? They've taken a hit and they're frightened—No, they're worse than frightened, they're pissed off— And thank God they are—What do you want? To be running around with your head in a bandage trying to find out which way Mecca is?

TALBOT: I'm not going to fight with you about it—How are you?

MAX: Me? I'm fine. The divorce came through, the kids hate me, my girlfriend ran off with a Byron Bay surfer and the Faculty's just closed my Department—How do you think I am? I'm terrific.

TALBOT: So how come they closed the Department?

MAX: What do you think? It's the same user pays shit all over the world—Economic Irrationalism—You remember that saying: 'When they took away the Jews, I said nothing because I wasn't a Jew'?—Yeah, well, they should update it to: 'When they took away the Latin Department, I said nothing because I wasn't a pederast'—You should see it, mate, it's fucked.

TALBOT: Fucked?

MAX: Sure—You can't run a course unless it's full of Asian millionaires' sons, and you can't keep 'em unless you pass the bastards no matter what they do—There's people running around out there designing bridges—this is no joke—and they can't even read standards manuals—It's like the whole country—the whole of Australia—has become one big joke—you know, a pretend country, like Fiji or the Solomon Islands: there's a police force, there's an army, there's even theatre companies putting on plays by important people like Shakespeare and Beckett, but basically the whole thing's fucked. The cops are corrupt, the army couldn't shoot its way out of a games arcade and the plays—well, who cares about the plays—I mean, it's just stuffed.

TALBOT: And that's why you're here?

MAX: Shit, mate, you've got it made: an American wife, residency, teaching position in one of the most prestigious universities in the US—What I wouldn't do to be you.

TALBOT: [*tongue in cheek*] But you know, Max, I still don't feel happy.

MAX: Fuck that—you must be earning shitloads.

TALBOT: More than you could imagine.

MAX: And whatever your political feelings might be about George W, you got to admit he's got the same attitude to taxation as the rest of us.

TALBOT: You know, Max, I just never thought about it that way.

MAX: This is a great place, Talbot; a great country. You feel real in a place like this, don't you reckon?

TALBOT: You're only saying that because you're visiting. No one here feels real, that's why they're so desperate to prove it to one another.

MAX: I don't reckon. I reckon they feel real because they are real; because when America says something, people listen; because when America wants something, they get it. Australia's finished, mate, we're fucked. The abos ran the place for sixty thousand years and it only took us two hundred to root it. We've had the longest drought in our history—you know that?—the longest drought—and the Government still doesn't believe in Global Warming. It's fucked, mate; we're fucked.

Light change.

◆ ◆ ◆ ◆ ◆

SCENE FOUR

Talbot's rooms.

TALBOT *looks quite scholarly as he stands, absorbed in a book, making notes on the edges with a pencil as he reads. The sound of a knock at the door hardly disturbs him.*

TALBOT: Yes...?

> *There's no answer.* TALBOT *continues reading, bending to cross-reference with something in another book. There's another knock, which he ignores in the same way.*

Yes...?

> *Again nothing. He starts looking around for something under the papers. This is the absent-minded professor par excellence. Another knock.*

Yes, come in...

> *He continues to potter about, not paying any attention as* MARGURITE *slowly enters the inner sanctum, the holy of holies, the Professor's rooms.*

Just take the bin; you can clean up later.

MARGURITE: Professor Finch?

> TALBOT *looks and is bewildered to see a young Asian girl in his room.*

TALBOT: Yes...?

MARGURITE: Margurite, Professor; Margurite Lee—I spoke to you yesterday.

TALBOT: Oh, yes, Margurite—Do you want something?

MARGURITE: I just wanted to see if I could have a few moments with you—I'm sure it won't take too long.

TALBOT: See me? Why? Did you make an appointment? The Secretary didn't mention anything about seeing a student.

MARGURITE: Please, Professor, it won't take too long—just a few minutes—

TALBOT: I'm rather busy, Miss Lee—

MARGURITE: [*noting*] Margurite—Look at all these books—Marx, Chomsky, Hobsbawm—Have you read his new one—the autobiography?

TALBOT: No—

MARGURITE: [*continuing to note*] Foucault—*Discipline and Punish* was good, and *The History of Sexuality*, but don't you think that post-modernism has had its day?—Have you read Klaus Thewlett's work on Nazi eroticism?

TALBOT: No—

MARGURITE: It's good to see no Baudrillard there—I couldn't stand him telling me one more time that the war on Iraq is only happening in the simulacrum, could you?

TALBOT: No.

MARGURITE: I'm very pleased to meet you, Professor; I love your lectures; if there were no reason to come to university other than to listen to you, I'd still come.

TALBOT: Thank you.

MARGURITE: I think you're great.

TALBOT: Yes… well… Did you leave the door open?

MARGURITE: Door?

TALBOT: Listen, Miss—

MARGURITE: Margurite.

TALBOT: Listen, Margurite, you're probably aware that there are very strict rules governing the interaction of staff and students—

MARGURITE: Oh, I didn't mean—

TALBOT: No, of course not—

MARGURITE: No—I just wanted to—I need to— [*She scrabbles in her bag for something.*] It's the question, see, the question… [*She pulls out a piece of paper, and reads.*] 'In the course of the Iran-Contra Inquiry, Lt-Colonel Oliver North testified that when engaged in their patriotic duty, the President and those who serve him cannot properly be held responsible within the law. Discuss this view and its relationship to contemporary democratic theory.'

TALBOT: Yes?

MARGURITE: Well, it just seems to me to be a very obtuse question.

TALBOT: Obtuse?

MARGURITE: Yes, I mean it was blatantly clear that Oliver North was a criminal funding the mass importation of cocaine into the United States with the full knowledge of the CIA—So what?

TALBOT: So what?

MARGURITE: Well, I mean, the CIA was in the throes of overthrowing the legitimate government of Nicaragua, they were assassinating government ministers, they were murdering innocent peasants and their children—Doesn't that count? What's it matter if they're importing cocaine in CIA planes?—that's the least reprehensible of their crimes.

TALBOT: I see your point—

MARGURITE: And what's crime got to do with it, anyhow? All law is is the legitimisation of power. Oliver North got off scot-free, a respected and celebrated member of society with his own TV show. John Poindexter's disciples are bugging your emails right now. Who cares what's legal or illegal, what matters is power and how it's used.

TALBOT: I think what I was trying to do—

MARGURITE: I mean, look at these books, Professor: political theory has advanced considerably beyond the question of whether or not America is a democracy—No one believes that, not even the voters! What people want to know is how power is being manipulated, and by whom, and what they can do about it. Those are the questions we should be addressing, not whether or not Ollie North ruffled a few feathers in Congress—Congress, Professor—Have you seen the sorts of clowns they're putting into Congress now? The Senate Majority Leader wanted to bring back segregation! Are you serious?

TALBOT: I see...

MARGURITE: Well, I don't mean, Are you serious?—I know you're serious—what I mean is, your course has been so much more interesting than that, and I wonder if I've just missed something in your essay question.

TALBOT: Look—

MARGURITE: Margurite.

TALBOT: Margurite—My course is just one small component of the Liberal Arts course of the MBA Degree program. Business Administration. Most of the students doing my course don't even attend lectures—

MARGURITE: But I do.

TALBOT: It's just a few credit points on their way to a hundred-thousand-dollar-a-year CEO position. If I can get them even thinking about what democracy is, I've achieved more than I thought I would.

MARGURITE: But that's not fair; that's not fair, Professor. I do come to your lectures and I do love thinking about these things and at the end of you opening up all these wonderful worlds for me—all these beautiful ideas—of truth and intellectual daring—of Galileo!—I don't want to have to dumb myself down to dissect Oliver North's clearly treasonable and profoundly confused ideas about what the role of a soldier in a modern democracy is just to get a pass and move on to a great career screwing people.

TALBOT: Well, I'm glad you appreciate Galileo.

MARGURITE: Yes! The great thinkers! Galileo! Bruno! People who stood and burnt for the truth—

TALBOT: Well, Galileo didn't exactly burn—

MARGURITE: And that's what I want to do, Professor! I want to think! And read! And write! I want to write great books, like these books, and I want to change people's lives—I want to do things, Professor—I want to change things. I want to be the voice of my generation; I want to be the one to solve the ecological crisis; I want to be the one that saves Africa from the banks—When I look back on my life, I want to see that I've done good and brought happiness where evil and misery flourished. That's what I want to do; isn't that what you want to do?

TALBOT: Yes. I suppose.

MARGURITE: You suppose?

TALBOT: Everyone tries—I'm writing.

MARGURITE: You're writing?

TALBOT: I've written a book; it's about to be published—Just a little—

MARGURITE: A book? Can I read it?

TALBOT: Read it? Sure.

MARGURITE: See, that's what I mean: what you're doing is good—teaching, thinking—you're good.

TALBOT: I don't think I'm good, Margurite.

MARGURITE: Well, I do. I think you're good. I think you're wonderful.

TALBOT: You'd like to read my book?

MARGURITE: Yes!

TALBOT: All right.

MARGURITE: Can I?

TALBOT: Why not?

   Light change.

◆ ◆ ◆ ◆ ◆

SCENE FIVE

Talbot's home.

EVE *is working at the computer in the shadows as* TALBOT *pours himself a drink.*

TALBOT: I heard a student today tell me she wanted to be the voice of her generation.

EVE: Was she pretty?

TALBOT: I was amazed.

EVE: Did you phone your publisher? He called again.

TALBOT: I hadn't heard anyone say anything like that for a while.

EVE: Maybe you should get her tested for drugs.

TALBOT: Do you remember when you wanted to be the voice of your generation?

EVE: Sure.

TALBOT: What happened to us, Eve?

EVE: When did the rot start, you mean?

TALBOT: Yes.

EVE: Didn't Brecht say you could change with your last breath?

TALBOT: My last breath?

EVE: You can change now, if you want. What do you want to change?

TALBOT: What do you want to change?

EVE: I asked you first.

TALBOT: Change? God, everything—Look at it: the place is a mess. You know, when the Cold War finished and the Soviet Union fell everyone thought great, now we can just get on with making it a better world, but instead of that it's like the dogs of capitalism have just been unleashed and are running wild right across the globe. Shit, Eve, it's like the bad old days of the Ugly American are back: we're still overthrowing governments in Latin America, murdering people in their beds; we've got a string of prisons dotted across the world filled with people who'll never be charged with any offence and we've got an intelligence service breathing so closely down everyone's necks we might as well call it a police state. What the fuck happened?

EVE: Look across the bay, Talbot...

TALBOT: No, that's wrong. Those terrorist attacks—You know how many people were killed in car accidents last year? Forty-three thousand. How come we're not launching a pre-emptive strike on Detroit? All this shit about terrorists is bullshit—They exist, sure they exist, but they exist because we made them, and everything we do to get rid of them just makes more of them.

EVE: You don't have to convince me.

TALBOT: I'd like to change all of that.

EVE: I thought you lot had.

TALBOT: No. It's like there's something deeper, isn't there? For all the froth and noise, for all the chanting and singing, nothing changed. A bit more personal freedom, a public acknowledgment of racism; a couple of seasons of flares and chunky shoes, and then slowly, almost imperceptibly being pulled back into the same groove, the same channel, like some current we were unaware of was moving us all in the same direction the whole time, but instead of resisting it now, all I feel is a bitter, kind of cynical detachment from the whole thing—

EVE: Yes.

TALBOT: And that's what shocked me listening to that kid. 'I want to be the voice of my generation.' It was so clear, so pure. And it made me realise how dirty I'd become.

EVE: I don't think you're dirty. I think you're compromised, but I'm compromised, too. We've made our compromise with the State. We've found a way to live, Talbot.

TALBOT: I'm okay—This is getting too maudlin—I'm not looking to get cheered up—We changed. People change. I still hate the cunts, but I guess I just don't think killing them is the right answer anymore—You know what I think?

EVE: What?

TALBOT: The only real and substantial change for the better that came about in the last century came about through non-violence.

EVE: What does that mean? Are you going to become a Buddhist now?

TALBOT: Do you still love me, Eve?

EVE: I think we've got some things to sort through.

TALBOT: Like what?

EVE: Like who we are and where we're going. I want a baby, Talbot; you know I want a baby. That was part of the deal.

TALBOT: Yes.

EVE: But it's no good if you don't want it, too. I thought you wanted it, Talbot, because I'm ready. Whether or not it's a police state, I'm ready, and I mean it. I'm tired of living my life in the eternals. I'm here, now, and I have needs and desires that are important to me. You know that; I know you do, so all I'm saying to you is that there's stuff to be sorted through.

TALBOT: Sure.

EVE: Do you love me?

TALBOT: Yes.

EVE: Do you?

TALBOT: Yes, I do. I do love you, Eve.

EVE: You loved your other wife, too.

TALBOT: And what?

EVE: And you left her.

TALBOT: I'm not leaving you.

EVE: You know, one day someone's going to make one of my movies, and it's going to be a great movie and people are going to see that movie and say, 'That Eve Finch, she's a great writer', and I don't know if that'll make me the voice of my generation, but it'll make me something, and I want that, too, Talbot; I want that desperately.

I want to say things that'll make people say, 'I never thought anyone else felt that way.' I want to say things that'll make people less afraid. I'm an idealist, too, Talbot; and so are you. We're both idealists because that's the only way you can live in a world like this.

Light change.

◆ ◆ ◆ ◆ ◆

SCENE SIX

Talbot's rooms.

A man in a hat and coat is loitering on the edge of the light when TALBOT *swings into view carrying his briefcase.*

MAN: Professor...?

TALBOT *looks.*

TALBOT: Yes?

MAN: I wonder if I could see you? It won't take a minute.

TALBOT: What do you want?

MAN: Let's not talk out here in the corridor—I think what I have to say will interest you.

TALBOT: How did you get in here?

MAN: Is this your room here? Do you mind if I come in?

TALBOT: Who are you?

Light change.

The MAN *enters and looks around.*

MAN: Ah, nice...

TALBOT *follows.*

TALBOT: I'm sorry, you're not a student, are you?

MAN: As a matter of fact I am, Professor; a student of life.

TALBOT: How did you get in? Normally you have to go through Security—

MAN: It must give you a great sense of security working in a place like this—Panelled walls—What's that? Walnut? Heritage, that's what it is, isn't it? Tradition.

TALBOT: I must insist you tell me who you are, otherwise I will have to ask you to leave.

MAN: Well, that's nice; that's nicely put; but then again, you're English.

TALBOT: What do you want?

MAN: No, you're not English, are you?—You're Australian.

> As TALBOT *reaches for the phone, the* MAN *pulls a gun out and points it at him.*

I wouldn't do that.

> TALBOT *puts the phone down.*

No, you've really got it made here—A distinguished professor in a nice ivy-league university—Do you get to fuck any of your students, Professor? What's the going rate nowadays? A grope for a pass and a blow-job for a credit? That the way things happen around here?

TALBOT: No.

MAN: No? Things must have changed since I went to university.

TALBOT: So that's how you achieved the great heights you've obviously scaled.

> *The* MAN *pistol whips him.*

MAN: Why don't you just shut the fuck up?

> TALBOT *flinches away.*

TALBOT: [*groaning*] Owwww…

MAN: Oh, the Professor's hurt—poor Professor—let me see—

TALBOT: Leave me alone!

MAN: Oh, he's pissed himself—Has he pooped himself, too? Poor Professor—That's pain, Professor, see, that's pain: that's good.

TALBOT: What the fuck do you want?

> *The* MAN *pistol whips him again.*

MAN: [*roaring*] No bad language, you dead cunt, or I'll kill you!

> TALBOT *again reels away.*

TALBOT: Fuck!

> *The* MAN *points the gun directly at* TALBOT*'s head.*

MAN: Shut up! Shut up, you deadshit; or you'll suck this bullet right into your cock-sucking brain.

> *Jesus H Christ, what the fuck is going on?*
>
> *Pause. The* MAN *glances about.*

You like reading, do you? I like reading, too. I like Jackie Collins.
What do you like? Marx? Groucho or Chico? Well, you'll have to get
rid of that, won't you?—Who are these deadshits? Adorno—
Hegel—Fuck—throw them out—throw them all out. The next time
I come here, I want to see nothing but Jackie Collins—*Deadly
Embrace* is a good one—Have you read *Deadly Embrace*?
Hollywood Wives is pretty good, too. In fact I'm sure you'd like
them all.

TALBOT: Help! Help!

MAN: Shut up, shit-for-brains, or I'll cut your tongue out.

    Pause.

TALBOT: Who the hell are you?

MAN: Listen, dickhead, there's one thing you've got to know about me:
I'm the one who asks the questions.

    A slight pause.

TALBOT: Okay.

MAN: Good. Sit down.

    TALBOT *does.*

Have you ever seen me before?

TALBOT: No.

MAN: Do you know who I am?

TALBOT: No.

MAN: Who do you think I am?

TALBOT: I have absolutely no idea.

MAN: Come on, dickhead: you're supposed to be a thinker, so think:
who am I?

TALBOT: I don't know—the father of one of the students.

MAN: The father of one of the students—interesting—And why would
the father of one of your students be pointing a gun at you? A female
student, perhaps—

TALBOT: Who are you?

    The MAN *again strikes* TALBOT, *who staggers back.*

Oh…

MAN: You're not listening, Professor, but I think you should: I am your
judge and jury, but you can think of me as your confessor, and what
you have to understand about me is that I know everything there is

to know about you already, so technically, I'm not here to find anything out, what I'm here to do is to facilitate your return to reality.

TALBOT: My return to reality?

MAN: That's right, and though I know all you're thinking at the moment is who is this madman, and how can I humour him long enough to get out of here alive?—though I know these are the questions running through your mind, you'll soon understand how wrong such musings are, and how your journey is inward, ever inward till you purge yourself of the poison that is destroying your soul.

TALBOT: Yes...?

MAN: You know, you're a very stupid man, Professor—It's a remarkable indictment of our society that a man as stupid as you could become a teacher responsible for the education of young people.

TALBOT: You have an interest in the education of young people. Naturally.

MAN: Don't think, Professor, that because I'm talking to you that I'm not going to kill you. I am going to kill you; I'm going to kill you slowly, and with considerable brutality, and whether I do it today, or this evening, or maybe even if I did it yesterday is of no real consequence, and all I'm offering you is your chance to retrieve a little of your dignity and confess.

TALBOT: Confess?

MAN: Yes, Professor, confess.

TALBOT: Confess? To what?

MAN: Someone must have been telling lies about Professor F, for without having done anything wrong he was arrested one fine morning.

TALBOT: What? What are you talking about? What's that?

MAN: Nice talking to you, Professor—'Bye.

The MAN *begins to move off into the shadows.*

TALBOT: Stop! Who are you? What do you want?

MAN: And don't forget: I'll be back.

Light change.

JACK'*s explosive voice suddenly ushers in.*

JACK: Talbot! This is terrible! Look at you! Where's the nurse?

TALBOT *is holding a bloody handkerchief to his forehead.*

TALBOT: What I want to know is how he got in.

JACK: Well, I want to know more than that, I can tell you—Was he black?

TALBOT: No.

JACK: So he took your wallet?

TALBOT: No, he didn't take anything.

JACK: What? Did you disturb him?

TALBOT: I think he might have been a parent.

JACK: A parent, Talbot…?

> *A uniformed* SECURITY *guy comes in.* JACK *immediately turns to him.*

Well?

> *The* SECURITY *guy says something low and indistinct that we cannot hear.*

TALBOT: How did he get a gun through the metal detector?—I thought those things were supposed to—

JACK: [*to the* SECURITY *guy*] What? Are you sure?

> TALBOT *hears the disbelief in* JACK'*s voice, and asks…*

TALBOT: What…?

> JACK *turns to the* SECURITY *guy.*

JACK: Tell him.

> *The* SECURITY *guy seems uncomfortable as he turns to* TALBOT.

SECURITY: There's no one on the tape.

TALBOT: Tape? What tape?

JACK: The videotape.

TALBOT: What's that mean?

SECURITY: There's no one on the tape, sir. There was no intrusion.

TALBOT: There was no intrusion? Are you out of your mind? [*Referring to his wounds*] What do you think this is?

JACK: [*to* TALBOT] All right, all right, calm down, Talbot— [*To the* SECURITY *guy*] You're sure—

SECURITY: I've gone through all the tapes—

TALBOT: Well, it must have been—You take photographs of people coming in when they sign on—

SECURITY: No…

TALBOT: Well then, he didn't come through any of the entrances, did he?—That's what it must be—he must have broken in through one of the windows.

SECURITY: I've checked that, and there were no break-ins.

TALBOT: Well, how would I know? It's not my job to work it out. You tell me: how did an armed man get past that great wall of useless human flesh—?

JACK: All right, Talbot—

TALBOT: What did he do? Just materialise?

JACK: [*to the* SECURITY *guy*] Thank you, Frank—

SECURITY: I can show him, sir.

JACK: Thank you, Frank—Just leave it with me.

The SECURITY *guy moves off as* TALBOT *repeats...*

TALBOT: Fuck!

JACK: Pull yourself together, Talbot; and I'd appreciate you keeping your bad language to yourself.

TALBOT: Bad language? I have just been mugged by an armed man in my own room. It is your responsibility as Head of the Department to ensure the safety of your staff. My safety has not been ensured.

JACK: If you're threatening legal action, I'd be careful to get my facts straight.

TALBOT: I'm not threatening legal action, Jack, I'm just telling you what happened—Jesus Christ, do you think I mugged myself?

JACK: If there has been a security lapse, I'll make sure we get to the bottom of it—Have you—done anything—said anything—that might have annoyed a parent?

TALBOT: No.

JACK: All right, Talbot, there's only two of us here—Have you had any kind of—sexual—?

TALBOT: No.

JACK: There's nothing I should know about between you and any of the students?

TALBOT: No.

JACK: You haven't had any student here in your room?

TALBOT: No.

JACK: You're being truthful with me; you're telling me the truth?

TALBOT: Look, there was...

JACK: What?

TALBOT: There was a student here yesterday.

JACK: There was a student here in your room yesterday.

TALBOT: Nothing happened—it was nothing, Jack…

JACK: Male or female?

TALBOT: Female—She wanted to talk about an essay question.

JACK: So it was organised by the Department Secretary? It's in your diary?

TALBOT: No. She just turned up.

JACK: Uh-huh—She just turned up—And you, of course, told her she had to make an appointment.

TALBOT: I did, Jack; I did.

JACK: But you talked to her anyhow…

TALBOT: Yes.

JACK: For how long?

TALBOT: A few minutes.

JACK: How long Talbot?

TALBOT: I don't know—thirty, forty minutes.

JACK: You had an unscheduled and unsupervised private meeting in your room with a female student for forty minutes.

TALBOT: I didn't do anything…

JACK: And what might this student's name be, Talbot?

TALBOT: Lee. Margurite Lee.

JACK: Margurite Lee. Do you happen to know who Margurite Lee's father is?

TALBOT: No.

JACK: Well, let me tell you. Margurite Lee's father just happens to be one of Singapore's wealthiest and one of the largest manufacturers of semi-conductors in the world. Margurite Lee herself hardly goes anywhere without her bodyguard. If Miss Lee visited you privately in your rooms yesterday, I have no doubt Mr Lee would have known about it last night.

TALBOT: Nothing happened…

JACK: There are protocols governing contact between staff and students, and they're as much for your protection as theirs—I think it would be in your best interests to fill out a Statutory Declaration stating precisely what happened between you and Miss Lee yesterday, and submit it to the Department Secretary as soon as possible.

TALBOT: This wasn't my fault—what happened to me was not my fault.

JACK: I think you should take the rest of the day off—Have you got any lectures? We can get a temp in—What about that friend of yours? Max? Is he up to it?

TALBOT: Sure—he said something.

JACK: Who did?

TALBOT: The guy—the mugger—as he was leaving. He said something.

JACK: What did he say?

TALBOT: I don't know—I can't remember—it was like 'Someone must have been telling lies about Professor F'—

JACK: 'Someone must have been telling lies about Professor F'?

TALBOT: Yes.

JACK: '... for without having done anything wrong he was arrested one fine morning.'

TALBOT: Yes—How did you know...?

JACK: It's Kafka—*The Trial*—it's the opening line of *The Trial*.

TALBOT: What trial?

JACK: Franz Kafka's *The Trial*—it's the opening line of Franz Kafka's *The Trial*—Of course, it's Joseph K, not Professor F, but that's what it is.

TALBOT: What would he be quoting *The Trial* to me for?

JACK: Well, you remember what happens to Joseph K in the end, don't you?

TALBOT: No—What?

JACK: He gets killed.

TALBOT: Killed? Why?

JACK: Well, that's the point of the book, Talbot: he never finds out.

    Light change.

◆ ◆ ◆ ◆ ◆

SCENE SEVEN

Talbot's home.

EVE *enters.*

EVE: Well, you're home early—What are you doing here?

    TALBOT *has his back turned to her.*

TALBOT: I decided to take the afternoon off.

EVE: Well, I wish you'd told me earlier—Do you want to see a movie? *Citizen Kane*'s showing over at the Film Forum.

TALBOT: No, I don't feel like seeing a movie.

EVE: There's something wrong with the car—I had trouble— [*But she notices.*] What's that? What happened to your face?

TALBOT: I fell.

EVE: Fell?

TALBOT: Down some stairs.

EVE: Show me—Talbot…

He turns away.

TALBOT: It's all right.

EVE: Have you been to the doctor? Do you want to go and see Paul?

TALBOT: No, I just want to be quiet.

EVE: Do you want me to get you something? Have you had lunch?

TALBOT: I'm all right, Eve.

EVE: Hey, you don't have to be a great big macho man for me; I never wanted to marry Crocodile Dundee.

TALBOT: I'm all right.

EVE: I'll leave you alone, then…

TALBOT: I'll just read; I've got some reading to catch up on.

EVE: I had a meeting; they liked the pitch.

TALBOT: That's good.

EVE: These guys are real—they're not like the other ones: they like my story; they don't want to turn it into *Spiderman*.

TALBOT: That's good.

EVE: I've got another *CSI* gig—The network liked my ep.

TALBOT: That's good.

EVE: I'll leave you to it, then…

TALBOT: Okay.

EVE: How did you fall down some stairs?

TALBOT: I tripped.

EVE: You ought to be more careful.

TALBOT: Yeah.

EVE: You're not angry with me, are you?

TALBOT: Have you ever read *The Trial*?

EVE: Sure—haven't you?

TALBOT: You know I don't have time to read fiction—What's it about?

EVE: It's about a man trying to escape his guilt.

TALBOT: What's he guilty of?

EVE: Of being a man.

TALBOT: Is that all?

EVE: Yes, that's all: of being a man.

   Light change.

◆ ◆ ◆ ◆ ◆

SCENE EIGHT

Security room.

A time-coded security video is playing on a large screen as TALBOT *stands underneath, watching.*

SECURITY: So that's your corridor, right?

TALBOT: Yes.

SECURITY: There's you going in.

TALBOT: That's not the right date.

SECURITY: Yes, it is: there's the date and time there in the corner—It happened yesterday, right?

TALBOT: Yes.

SECURITY: So where's the guy? There's you going in and then there's Professor—

   We see JACK *rushing in.*

TALBOT: Wait, there's a jump there—

SECURITY: It's been edited.

TALBOT: But I want to see the original tape.

SECURITY: Nothing happens for three hours, Professor.

TALBOT: I want to see it.

   STAN *wanders in.*

STAN: So what are you guys up to?

TALBOT: Stan.

STAN: Heard you were down here—How's it going?

TALBOT: It's an edited tape, Stan; I want to see the original.

STAN: Is there any problem with that, Frank?

SECURITY: No problem, sir; I've just got more to do with my time than sit here watching blank tape for three hours.

STAN: I'm sure Talbot can be trusted to watch the tape himself, Frank.

TALBOT: What am I going to do? Draw the intruder in myself?

The SECURITY *guy moves off.*

STAN: So have you got that statement?

TALBOT: Yes—yes—here, Stan—

He hands STAN *a piece of paper.*

You believe me, don't you?

STAN: Sure.

TALBOT: I mean, why would I report something that didn't happen?

STAN: No idea.

TALBOT: Well, I wouldn't, Stan—I didn't.

STAN *glances at the Statutory Declaration.*

STAN: Have you ever been accused of this before, Talbot?

TALBOT: Accused of what?

STAN: You didn't touch the girl?

TALBOT: No…

STAN: [*referring to the Stat Dec*] And this is a truthful account of what took place between you and—whatever her name is.

TALBOT: Yes.

STAN: I'm just the lawyer, right, Talbot…?

TALBOT: Yes…

STAN: If I were you, I'd be really careful about this sort of thing.

TALBOT: What sort of thing?

A new tape begins as the SECURITY *guy returns.*

SECURITY: Okay, there it is, and I've put on the day before's as well, just to be really sure—Make yourself comfortable, Professor…

TALBOT: [*to* STAN] I didn't do anything—I was bashed; I was bashed in the university.

STAN *sees* MARGURITE *entering Talbot's rooms.*

STAN: Hmmm, she's nice…

TALBOT: I was bashed, I tell you; I was bashed.

STAN: I hope it was worth it…

Light change.

◆ ◆ ◆ ◆ ◆

SCENE NINE

University hall.

A security warning booms through the stillness.

SECURITY: [*voice-over*] All unattended bags and parcels will be destroyed. Leave no personal belongings unattended.

> *As* TALBOT *has his briefcase in his hand and is on his way to his rooms, a voice calls...*

MARGURITE: Professor...?

TALBOT: Oh, Margurite...

> MARGURITE *runs cheerfully on.*

MARGURITE: Hi, Professor—I was just wondering if you'd had a chance to get me a copy of the book yet?

TALBOT: The book? Look, Margurite—

MARGURITE: You were going to give me a copy of your book to read—remember?

TALBOT: Yes, but...

MARGURITE: I was thinking about what you said, Professor, and it was just so inspirational—I'd love you to talk to our reading group—We're studying Marcuse at the moment—Do you like Marcuse?—*Eros and Civilization*—I think we've badly misunderstood all that sexual liberation stuff.

TALBOT: I'm sure—Margurite, does your father know about me?

MARGURITE: My father?

TALBOT: Have you talked to your father about me?

MARGURITE: No.

TALBOT: Margurite—Miss Lee—please—you have to understand—I think it's important that we keep our relationship professional.

MARGURITE: Relationship?

TALBOT: I understand, and I appreciate, that you have a strong interest in politics—

MARGURITE: What's my father got to do with anything?

TALBOT: I just want things to be right between us—do you understand?

MARGURITE: Has my father done something?

TALBOT: Do you understand?

MARGURITE: What's happened?

TALBOT: Do you understand, Miss Lee?

MARGURITE: No, I don't; what's happened?

TALBOT: Nothing's happened.

MARGURITE: Did he have someone bash you?

TALBOT: No. Nothing, Margurite—really.

MARGURITE: Then who?

TALBOT: Really, it's just a question of being professional.

MARGURITE: I thought you were a socialist...

TALBOT: I'm a teacher.

MARGURITE: I thought you were a revolutionary.

TALBOT: I'm a teacher, Miss Lee—I've got to go; I really must.

MARGURITE: I thought we were comrades; I thought you understood.

TALBOT: Please, Miss Lee; you have to understand.

MARGURITE: No, I don't understand, Professor—I thought you were
    different to the others; I thought you actually believed in what you
    said!

TALBOT: I have a responsibility.

MARGURITE: Who to?

TALBOT: Goodbye, Miss Lee.

MARGURITE: What did he do to you?!

> *Light change.*

◆ ◆ ◆ ◆ ◆

SCENE TEN

Talbot's rooms.

As TALBOT *enters,* MAX *notices his face.*

MAX: Shit, mate, what happened to you?

> TALBOT *is scrabbling around in his briefcase for something
> and has forgotten what he looks like.*

TALBOT: What?

> MAX *gestures to his face.*

Oh... an accident...

MAX: I didn't realise they took academic arguments quite so seriously over here.

TALBOT *ignores the remark and hands* MAX *some forms.*

TALBOT: Here's the Green Card application—All you need's sponsorship and you'll be fine.

MAX: I can't tell you how much I appreciate this, Talbot—And you think...

TALBOT: Jack.

MAX: ... 'll play ball?

TALBOT: I might not do it through Jack—I might go directly to the Dean.

MAX: You've got my resume, haven't you?—I'm writing a book, too, did you know that?

TALBOT: You're writing a book? What about?

MAX: Well, I'm researching a book—I haven't actually started writing yet—but I don't think it'll take me long when I get down to it.

TALBOT: What's it about?

MAX: Oh, you know, security, intelligence, that sort of thing.

TALBOT: Intelligence?

MAX: Sort of—sort of a postmodern—

TALBOT: Postmodern?

MAX: You know—does the State exist?—That sort of thing—something for the CV.

TALBOT: I didn't know you were interested.

MAX: Everybody's interested, aren't they?

TALBOT: You know, that's the thing I'm finding most fascinating at the moment.

MAX: What's that?

TALBOT: How prescient Eisenhower's speech was.

MAX: Oh, yes—Which speech was that?

TALBOT: The Military-Industrial Complex speech—the one he gave in '61.

MAX: Oh, yes. Mighty—What's the staff-student ratio around here?

TALBOT: I mean, that's what it's like, isn't it?—Every now and then you get a glimpse of it—the Security State, the Intelligence State— It's just there, just under the surface, waiting to break through.

MAX: What is?

TALBOT: Don't you think?

MAX: I don't know what you're talking about, mate.

TALBOT: The State, Max, the Intelligence State—isn't that what we're talking about? It's just like Eisenhower was saying: the Military-Industrial Complex is a threat to democracy and is taking over.

MAX: President Eisenhower said that?

TALBOT: Yes! I thought that's what you were saying?

MAX: Who? Me?

TALBOT: Then what?

MAX: I don't know—Geez—You know: old paradigms of socio-political cultural exchange obscuring the essence of the inessential bullshit-bullshit—you know—

TALBOT: What are you talking about, Max?

MAX: What are you talking about? It sounds like you're saying the intelligence services are taking over!

TALBOT: They are!

MAX: Where? Here?

TALBOT: Of course here—How else do you explain all this crap going on?

MAX: What crap?

TALBOT: Homeland Security—everyone running around duct-taping their windows shut—the scare campaign.

MAX: Scare campaign? They've got fucking terrorists running around trying to kill them—Are you out of your head?

TALBOT: That's not it.

MAX: What are you saying?

TALBOT: I'm saying Eisenhower was right: the Military-Industrial Complex is using the terrorist crisis to stage a takeover; that's what I'm saying.

MAX: Bullshit—Eisenhower said that? Bullshit—You're crazy, Talbot.

TALBOT: What are you lowering your voice for, Max?

MAX: Lowering my voice? Jesus Christ, didn't you hear what you just said?

TALBOT: I'm just saying what Eisenhower said forty years ago, Max!

MAX: Bullshit he did, and even if he did, who was he anyhow?

TALBOT: He was the fucking President of the United States, Max! A wartime president who'd actually fought in a war!

MAX: Talbot?! You're saying America is becoming a dictatorship.

TALBOT: Then you tell me what's happening!

MAX: Look, mate, I don't know what's happening—I just arrived here, right? And, all right, I know the Americans go on with all this flag-waving, patriotic bullshit and think the rest of the world hates them, but fuck, Talbot, they're right: the rest of the world does hate 'em—I hate 'em, and I want to live here! It's envy, isn't it: everyone looks at what they've got and wants it, only they don't want to put the hard work into it, do they; they don't want to dismantle their own fucked-up societies and build new ones—They don't want to get rid of all the old power elites and give individuals their own power; they don't want to educate women or stop sending kids blind weaving rugs, they just want the stuff, that's right, isn't it; and figure the reason they can't get the stuff, is because the Americans are stopping them. I mean, that's just the way the world works, isn't it?—Like in *The Life of Brian*—'What did the Romans ever do for us?' That's where we're at now, and now some prick's actually done something about it, and killed three thousand people, and the Americans are fucking mad as hell, because they know every single one of them is on that plane hurtling toward the Twin Towers and they don't like it and they're not going to stand for it, and they're going to get the pricks that're threatening them. Well, all power to George W—I don't want the fucking pricks to win, either. There were Aussies killed up there, mate, there were English, there were Scots, there were fucking Moslems, for fuck's sake! There was fucking everybody: everyone's hopes were up there in those two towers—Hopes for their own advancement, hopes that dumb human beings like us could actually get somewhere, hopes for a better world—and those deadshits—Osama and his mates—those fucking deadshits just went, Nah, we don't care about you and your hopes. Your God sucks. You're fucked. This is the way the world is now. Fuck ya. That's what they said. And now America's saying, Fuck you back, and if they didn't, mate, then I'd be scared. It's a war, Talbot—

TALBOT: It's not a war.

MAX: It is a war. It's a war against terror and it's a war against ignorance, and it's a war against prejudice and pure dumb-arsed fuckwittedness, and we've got to win that war, otherwise we're fucked.

TALBOT: It's not a war, Max, it's a determined and dedicated attack on every single legal and civil right from 'Habeas Corpus' and 'Innocent

Until Proven Guilty' down—It's an attack on eight hundred years of jurisprudence.

MAX: Look, Talbot, I don't think anyone even understands those sorts of high-falutin' ideas anymore; all anybody wants is not to be standing next to a suicide-bomber.

TALBOT: And the way we can ensure that is to hand the keys over to the same guys that have been corrupting America for the last thirty years? To the Watergate buggers? To the Iran-Contra criminals? I'm not crazy, Max, you are if you think any of these cop organisations give a flying fuck about your freedom or your safety or anything having to do with you. You know what you are to them? Potential collateral damage, that's what. No, actually, you're even less than that, because you're not even an American citizen. You know what they could do to you? Some spook in Washington could decide you're undesirable because they've mixed you up with someone somewhere else, or maybe in their eyes you really are undesirable. Maybe one time you subscribed to *Hustler* magazine, or you're a Quaker, or maybe you didn't say your prayers last night, and you could be abducted off the street, and disappeared into some hellhole where they could keep you for as long as they liked, and then they could take you out and shoot you for no other reason than that they don't know what else to do with you, and do you think the Australian Government would say boo about it? Do you think Alexander Downer's going to stand up for you? That's now, Max, that's not a speculation about what might happen in the future, that could happen now.

MAX: If that's the sort of thing you've been saying around the traps, no wonder your face looks the way it does—Is that what your book's about?

TALBOT: No—no, it's an historical study.

MAX: An historical study about what?

TALBOT: Weren't you listening the other night?

MAX: All that myth shit—Well, that's a real bestseller.

TALBOT: I didn't write it to be a bestseller.

MAX: So what's it called?

TALBOT: *Myth, Propaganda and Disaster in Nazi Germany and Contemporary America—A Comparative Study.*

   A slight pause.

MAX: Are you out of your mind?

> TALBOT *looks at him, sensing the man's bewilderment.*

TALBOT: What...?

MAX: *Myth, Propa*—What?

TALBOT: *Myth, Propaganda and Disaster*—

MAX: You're comparing America to Nazi Germany—Are you insane?

TALBOT: No—Why?

MAX: Why? Why?! Do you teach Politics or not?

TALBOT: It's an academic study—I can compare—

MAX: Academic study, Talbot? *Myth, Propaganda and Disaster in Nazi Germany and Saddam Hussein's Iraq*—yes!—that's a study—that makes sense—*Myth, Propaganda and Disaster in Nazi Germany and Tasmania*, for fuck's sake—even that's all right; but *Myth, Propaganda and Disaster in Nazi Germany and Contemporary America*?! Are you out of your cotton-picking mind?!

TALBOT: It's just a book.

MAX: Shit, mate, you don't get it, do you?

TALBOT: Get what?

MAX: Jesus Christ, Talbot, ten seconds ago you were telling me I could be dragged off the street and shot for being a Quaker, and you think you're going to get away with comparing the United States with Nazi Germany? Fuck, mate, where do you keep your head? It's changed, can't you see that? Everything's changed.

TALBOT: Don't you think academics have a responsibility to stand up for what they believe?

MAX: When was the last time you heard anybody standing up for anything other than a second serve?

TALBOT: Well, I am. I am standing up for what I believe in, and if I didn't, I don't know what I'd be.

MAX: Dean of the Faculty.

TALBOT: Fuck you, Max.

MAX: Well, I don't have to say fuck you back, Talbot, because you've well and truly fucked yourself. I hope you enjoy life at Wollongong University, because that's where you're headed, if you're lucky.

TALBOT: So this is how low Australian intellectual life has sunk.

MAX: Oh, spare me the martyr speech—'Here I stand, I cannot do otherwise'—Look, Talbot, nobody gives a flying fuck what we think because they're all too busy either kicking heads or pulling their heads in. You might think it's fun calling the guys with the guns deadshits, but it's not the sixties anymore, and they're not going to pat you on the head for sticking flowers in their rifles this time.

TALBOT: They weren't then, either, Max. They were shooting people.

MAX: Well, you just remember that, Talbot, because if the shit hits the fan, that's what they'll be doin' pretty soon again.

Light change.

◆ ◆ ◆ ◆ ◆

SCENE ELEVEN

Stan and Jill's apartment.

JILL *is trying on a hat in front of a mirror, as* STAN *wanders about in the background, as if they're in two completely different spaces.*

STAN: [*offstage*] What's this, sweetheart?

JILL: What's what? Come and tell me what you think of my new hat.

STAN: This five-hundred-dollar dinner bill at Washington Park—I can't even remember being at Washington Park.

JILL: Five hundred dollars? Is that the Amex bill?

STAN: Is this yours? Did you go to the Washington Park?

JILL: Amy and I went a couple of weeks ago.

STAN: Amy and you? I thought you didn't like her?

JILL: Oh, you know—girls—Do you think this suits me?—It's called 'A Breakfast at Tiffany's'—they're doing a remake. Madonna is going to play Audrey Hepburn.

STAN: Five hundred dollars, baby? What did you eat? The last white rhinoceros?

JILL: Do they serve white rhinoceros?

STAN: You got to be more careful, Jill; look at this stuff—How much are you spending?

JILL: We got carried away with the Dom Perignon.

STAN: You're not kidding—What were you doing? Having a bath?

JILL: It was just a couple of bottles—It's very over-rated, don't you think?

STAN: I wouldn't know—I've never been able to afford it. So what do you want to do? You want me to pick it up?

JILL: Yeah, why not? Would you mind, baby?

STAN: Shit, Jill—five hundred bucks.

JILL: Be a sweetheart, Stan.

STAN: I'll do it, honeybunch, but I think there's a blow-job in it for me, don't you?

JILL: More than one, smoochy-pooch.

STAN: Five hundred bucks, baby? I didn't think you could drink that much plonk.

JILL: Well, a girl's got to amuse herself somehow.

STAN: Why not have an affair? That'd probably be cheaper.

JILL: I don't think so—So what do you think? [*Mimicking*] 'I suppose you think I'm very brazen or *très fou* or something.'

STAN: No *fou*-er than anyone else—You know she was playing a hooker, don't you?

JILL: Who? Audrey? No—Audrey would never play a hooker.

STAN: Sure she was! Why do you think she says she gets fifty dollars to go to the powder room?

JILL: Audrey was? No—Really? Well, maybe Madonna could play her...

Light change.

◆ ◆ ◆ ◆ ◆

SCENE TWELVE

Talbot's rooms.

TALBOT *picks up the phone and dials.*

TALBOT: Hello? University Press? It's Talbot Finch here—Could I speak to the publisher...? He's not? When will he be back...? [*He looks at his watch.*] Look, tell him I rang, will you? It's about my book... Yes, my book. Could you please tell him to ring me—it's about my book.

He hangs up.

Light change.

◆ ◆ ◆ ◆ ◆

SCENE THIRTEEN

A *consulting room.*

A *woman* THERAPIST *is sitting in a chair, watching* EVE.

THERAPIST: So tell me.

EVE: I don't know; I don't know anymore.

THERAPIST: Do you think he loves you?

EVE: Yes. But it's not enough.

THERAPIST: What's not enough?

EVE: It's not enough to stop the hurt; it's not enough to save me.

THERAPIST: Save you?

EVE: Yes, save me; I want to be saved; I want my life to be saved, to be
given some meaning, and I know another person can't do that for
you, but I can't do it for myself. I can't, I've tried, but I can't.

THERAPIST: Is that why you feel so angry?

EVE: Angry? Do you think I feel angry?

THERAPIST: You sound angry.

EVE: Do I?

THERAPIST: Do you think it's my fault?

EVE: No.

THERAPIST: Do you think it's your husband's?

EVE: Do I sound angry?

THERAPIST: Yes.

EVE: I suppose I am angry, but it's so far down, I'm barely aware of it.
I hate this, this floundering. I read this thing the other day, about self
awareness—did you read it? That they're trying to write software
for machines to have self awareness—isn't that a strange idea?—
and the reason is to try to improve their mobility, because if a machine
isn't really aware where it is in an environment, then it can't really
navigate properly—So the idea is to write a program which allows
the machine to locate itself in an environment—and that's a kind of
self awareness; and so there I was thinking, is that all it is? All this
goo in the middle of us, all this—who am I, where am I going, what
does it mean?—all that stuff that's kept the motor of our civilization
going for the last three thousand years—is just so I can get from the
front door to the supermarket and back—And then I got a flash of

one of those endless repetitive things—one of those Escher moments as I saw myself seeing myself seeing myself, all of us caught in a kind of transparent sphere of consciousness expanding at the speed of light—And you just wonder, don't you?—is Douglas Adams right, and the answer is 42? Well, he'd know now, wouldn't he; or he wouldn't, he wouldn't if he's just gone to dust, gone to cosmic dust disappearing into the darkness, and if machines can locate themselves in an environment, will they start wondering what it all means, too? And when they break down and decay, will they rage against fate and feel betrayed and alone? Will they feel angry that something has given them the ability to locate themselves in an environment, but never told them why they're there?—Am I making sense? Is any of this making sense?

THERAPIST: Is it?

EVE: No. No, it doesn't make sense; and if tomorrow a little green man from outer space arrived in New York and addressed the United Nations and said, 'I'm here to tell you the reason why you're here, and the reason why you're here is that five billion years ago a superior intelligence planted you as part of a strategy to fight the eternal war against the despicable Trogs', that wouldn't make any sense either, because that's not the kind of sense we want.

THERAPIST: What sort of sense do we want?

EVE: To know who we are, to not feel so alone.

THERAPIST: Eve, I've noticed how frequently you relate those two things: knowing who you are and not feeling alone. Why do you do that?

    Pause. EVE *is quietly crying.*

    Eve…?

EVE: I'm sorry…

THERAPIST: Eve, you understand what you're doing, don't you? The thing you're craving is a kind of mystical union with the world, where there are no distinctions and no barriers, where you are me and we are one, and there's nothing especially wrong with that nostalgia for the kind of primal state where individuality is abandoned and you just surrender yourself to the mass—There's nothing terribly wrong with it, and it's the basis of all religion and most political movements— But you have to see how illusory it is, because the fact of the matter is, you are not me and we are not one, and a love that doesn't respect that is really a form of tyranny.

EVE: Yes…

THERAPIST: Is that what you want?

EVE: No, no I don't suppose it is.

THERAPIST: That's what being an adult is, isn't it: respecting boundaries, acknowledging limits.

EVE: Yes.

THERAPIST: Do you want to be an adult?

EVE: I suppose in some ways I don't. In some ways I'd prefer to be a child, and to have decisions made for me, and to be tucked into bed at night.

THERAPIST: Would you?

EVE: Isn't that America? Frightened of growing up, frightened of being different? Isn't that why we all run around covering ourselves with the flag and pointing our finger at anyone who isn't? All we want is to be children again; dangerous children, with our guns and our bombs and our feet-stamping demands to be loved. Maybe that's what it is. I'm not neurotic, I'm just American.

THERAPIST: You're not neurotic, Eve, you're just unhappy.

EVE: Why?

THERAPIST: For all the reasons you've given.

EVE: Have I given reasons?

THERAPIST: That you'll die, that you'll fail, that you don't understand why and that you're alone, even when you're with someone who loves you. They're the reasons you're unhappy; they're the reasons we're all unhappy.

EVE: Are we all unhappy?

THERAPIST: Yes, for some of the time, but for most of the time we're happy. But maybe there is a part of us that is always unhappy, Eve, the part that longs to be at one with the world.

EVE: Is that wrong?

THERAPIST: Well, if you don't mind handing your conscience over to someone else, no.

EVE: I want an America where people are happy, but not because they're all marching around calling each other sir, and not because they think they're one people under God; but because we're adult enough to face our frailties and admit our faults and live—yes, live—with the kind of people we are. I don't want an America gloating over a defeated world, lording it over everyone else, telling everyone how to live their lives, I just want to live in a community at peace with itself and humble enough to acknowledge when it's wrong. We used to be like that; people used to be like that. What happened to us? When did we become what we've become?

Light change.

◆ ◆ ◆ ◆ ◆

SCENE FOURTEEN

An underground garage.

As TALBOT *walks into the darkness, a voice challenges from behind.*

MAN: [*offstage*] Well, Professor—so nice to see you again...

TALBOT *turns and, recognising him, backs away.*

TALBOT: All right...

MAN: All right?

TALBOT: All right, I know who you are.

MAN: You know who I am, do you...?

TALBOT: And if this is the way you bodyguards behave on campus—

The MAN *points his gun at* TALBOT.

MAN: Shut up.

TALBOT: Look, fuck you, this is just a misunderstanding—She came to see me about an essay question.

MAN: Shut up, I said—

TALBOT: No, you shut up; and I don't appreciate having a gun pointed at me.

MAN: Better get used to it, dickbrain.

TALBOT: Look, I've told you what's going on, and that's the end of it— She's a student, that's all—she means nothing to me.

MAN: Get moving.

TALBOT: What are you talking about? She's a student.

MAN: Just shut the fuck up.

Light change.

END OF ACT ONE

ACT TWO

SCENE FIFTEEN

Talbot's rooms.

MAN: So, Professor, democracy… [*pulling down*] … and what's *Das Kapital* got to do with democracy?

TALBOT: All right, what's going on?

MAN: In fact, what's any of this got to do with democracy?

TALBOT: I demand you tell me what this is about.

MAN: In fact, what's any of this doing here at all? Didn't you believe me when I said all I wanted to see when I got back here was Jackie Collins?

TALBOT: Jackie Collins? What is this shit?

MAN: I'll tell you what this shit is, Professor—What say I start blowing off your fingers one by one till we work out what democracy is?— How about that, ay?

TALBOT: How dare you stand there with a gun in your hand threatening me and talking about democracy?

MAN: There's plenty of people with guns in their hands and strapped to their backpacks who want to talk about democracy, Professor—By the way, I fixed your car.

TALBOT: What did you say?

MAN: You heard. In fact, I think we're seeing the biggest expansion of democracy in fifty years.

TALBOT: Look, if this isn't about Margurite Lee, what is it about?

MAN: Margurite Lee? She's sounds nice. Who's she, Professor? Your current squeeze? Have you been a naughty professor, Professor?

TALBOT: All right, come on—what is this?

MAN: I thought you knew—Come on, Professor, who am I? Who am I, Mr Smart Guy—Mr *Das Kapital* in the Original German—Mr John Stuart Mill—who am I?

TALBOT: What do you want?!

MAN: You see the thing is, Professor, none of this means shit: these books, these ideas—None of it means shit to an Afghan peasant with both his feet blown off—None of it means shit, Professor, to a liquor store owner handing over his day's takings to a couple of fourteen-year-old niggers armed with a Saturday Night Special—None of it means shit.

TALBOT: What are you? Some sort of neo-Nazi—?

MAN: Does it? Answer me! None of it means shit! Your world doesn't mean shit!

TALBOT: This is my world!

MAN: And it's fucked.

TALBOT watches as the MAN prowls about.

Look at this place—the little nick-nacks, the kinds of honours and rewards you guys poke each other with—This is from another century, isn't it?—The last century.

TALBOT: Okay, so you've told me: you don't like me, you don't like my books, you wish the world was run by Rush Limbaugh—

The MAN suddenly has TALBOT's arm twisted up his back, making him yell in pain.

Aaaaggghhhh!

MAN: If you think I'm just some tobacco-chewing redneck, you've got another think coming—

He shoves him away.

Now get over there. I don't want to be that close to you—I don't want to have to smell you.

TALBOT watches him.

So tell me; I've got a question for you: when the plague is sweeping through the city, how do you stop it spreading? By carrying the victims to public hospitals and infecting everyone on the way, or by bricking them in, plague victims and their families alike, so the disease doesn't have a chance to escape?—Which is more important, Professor? The rights of the few, or the survival of the many?

TALBOT: I'm not going to talk to you—

MAN: Answer me!

TALBOT: This isn't a medieval city and we're not suffering from the plague!

MAN: How do you know? How do you fucking know? How do you know the Black Death isn't creeping through the Bronx right now? How do you know your neighbour isn't dying of pig fever next door?

TALBOT: I don't; but until I see it, I don't want to brick him and his wife in for fear that they are.

MAN: By the time you see it, Professor, you'll have it yourself.

TALBOT: You're none of those things, are you?—you're not a Nazi—

MAN: What are you, Professor, that's the question you should be asking.

TALBOT: Are you a government agent? Are you a cop?

MAN: Do you think I'm a cop, Professor? Have you been a bad boy?

TALBOT: You're mad.

MAN: You know, that's the first thing you've said that you actually mean.

TALBOT: Is that what you think? Is that what this is about? That this— War on the World—

MAN: War on Terrorism.

TALBOT: War on the World—You think this is going to get democracy back on track? Is that what this is about?

MAN: America. This is going to get America on track.

TALBOT: And save us all from the plague of liberalism…?

MAN: Frighteningly simple, isn't it, Professor?

TALBOT: You're fucking insane.

MAN: I didn't drive two planes into the World Trade Center, Professor, but now that someone did, I'm not the one trying to pretend nothing's changed—Who's insane?

TALBOT: You're threatening more damage to America than anything any Arab terrorist could do.

MAN: Who's worried about them? They're gone. It's you, Professor, you! You're the one we're worried about now.

TALBOT: Me? Why me? What did I do?!

MAN: Because it's people like you who opened the door and let them in. You're the disease, Professor; fuck you; fuck you; fuck you!

Light change.

◆ ◆ ◆ ◆ ◆

SCENE SIXTEEN

Max's hotel.

TALBOT *is upset.*

TALBOT: Jesus Christ, Max, what am I going to do?

MAX: Are you sure, Talbot? I mean, it does sound very strange.

TALBOT: Strange? Fuck!

MAX: You think this guy is—like—FBI or something?

TALBOT: I don't know—No—not FBI—he couldn't be FBI—he'd have to identify himself if he was—There's rules, Max; procedures; you just can't move into someone's life and start monstering them.

MAX: Well, no; but you're saying he has...

TALBOT: Yes!

MAX: You're not just—imagining—this, are you?

TALBOT: Imagining it? Max, this man threatened to kill me.

MAX: Kill you, Talbot?

TALBOT: Do I sound sane to you?

MAX: Well, frankly, no: you're upset, you're making these wild accusations—You don't sound sane, no.

TALBOT: I don't feel sane, I can tell you that. I thought I understood what was going on, that I'd imagined the worst, but I never imagined anything like this.

MAX: The worst, Talbot?

TALBOT: This is it, isn't it?—After they've kicked the shit out of the Arabs, it's time to turn the blowtorch on America.

MAX: Look, mate, if I thought that, I'd be shitting myself.

TALBOT: Maybe I am.

MAX: No, you're not. You're not grabbing your bag and heading for the nearest airport; I bet you're not even writing a letter to the editor about it. This is bullshit, Talbot; you don't believe that at all.

TALBOT: I'm not an American citizen, Max; I could be tried by a military tribunal.

MAX: Tried? What for?

TALBOT: I don't know what for—maybe that's what he meant.

MAX: That's what who meant?

TALBOT: The first time I met him, he quoted *The Trial* to me.

MAX: Kafka's *Trial*?

TALBOT: Yes.

MAX: What did he say?

TALBOT: The opening line—you know—'Someone must have—'

MAX: '—been telling lies about Joseph K—'

TALBOT: Yes.

MAX: '—for without having done anything wrong he was arrested one fine morning'—Is that it? Is that what he said to you?

TALBOT: Yes.

MAX: Well, that's it—there you go.

TALBOT: What do you mean?

MAX: Someone's denounced you.

TALBOT: Denounced me?

MAX: Someone's made an accusation against you, so all you have to do is find out what it is and refute it and Bob's your uncle.

TALBOT: Refute it? But I don't know what it is.

MAX: That's what I'm saying: find out what you're accused of, and you'll be right. You haven't done anything wrong, have you?

TALBOT: I don't know.

MAX: What do you mean, you don't know.

TALBOT: Well, what's wrong anymore?

MAX: Talbot, have you done anything you think might be wrong?

TALBOT: Fuck, Max…

MAX: Think, Talbot, think.

> *Light change.*

◆ ◆ ◆ ◆ ◆

SCENE SEVENTEEN

Jack's office.

JACK: So what do you think?

> STAN *moves out of the shadows, flicking through the paperwork.*

STAN: I think you've got him.

JACK: Got him?

STAN: You've done everything you're required to do. Maybe you should have insisted that he go to a doctor and get a proper medical examination, but as far as your legal responsibilities are concerned, you've ticked all the right boxes—I don't know what you're worried about.

JACK: So he can't sue.

STAN: Sure he can sue—anyone can sue—it's just that he'd be hard pressed to prove his case—He's seen the security tapes—What's he say about that?

JACK: He hasn't said anything.

STAN: That's because there's nothing he can say—Just make sure you hold onto them—I mean, they're the clincher, aren't they?—It never happened.

JACK: No.

STAN: It never happened, Jack; he made it up.

JACK: Yeah.

STAN: Say it, Jack. Say he made it up.

JACK: Why would he do that?

STAN: That's not our concern. If you believe he made the story up about being assaulted in his room, say it.

JACK: But what if he didn't? What if it happened?

STAN: What?

JACK: What if it happened, Stan? What if he was bashed?

STAN: You mean—with the girl? There was no girl there, either, Jack...

JACK: Look, I've been trying to think my way through this, trying to work it out, and the only thing that doesn't make sense is why he'd make something like that up in the first place—You didn't see him, Stan.

STAN: What are you saying?

JACK: What if he's not lying?

STAN: Am I missing something here?

JACK: Think about it, Stan: what if he was assaulted? What if someone got into his office and bashed him, just like he said they did.

STAN: How could they? You've seen the tape; I've seen the tape—

JACK: What if it's been faked? What then?

STAN: What if the tape's been faked? Who by? Who'd fake the tape?

JACK: What if there's a Security operation taking place here—right here now in the university—without our knowledge?

STAN: A Security operation? Who, Jack?

JACK: What if he's a terrorist, Stan?

STAN: Talbot?

JACK: Yes, Talbot; what if he's a terrorist—what if he's giving money to them, or something?

STAN: Jesus…

JACK: What if he's running a website, or a cell, like those pricks in Hamburg were—You've heard the way he talks—what if he's recruiting people?

STAN: Well, God, Jack, I don't know—Have you got any evidence? Anything to make you suspicious?

JACK: No—But you get it, don't you? A radicalism, a general inclination, a temperament…

STAN: Let me try to think this through—

JACK: How do you think this is going to look to the sponsors if one of our lecturers turns out to be a goddamn terrorist? I appointed him, Stan. Can't you see what I'm saying?

STAN: Oh…

JACK: Yes, oh! Price Waterhouse! AOL! We've got our annual dinner coming up at the Guggenheim in a couple of weeks—What do you think Lieberman is going to say if he finds out one of our lecturers is being investigated?

STAN: But you had a security check done on him.

JACK: So fucking what? We've had security checks on the whole fucking country and it's still crawling alive with the bastards—What am I going to do?

STAN: Get rid of him. Get rid of him as fast as you can. Pay him out if you have to, but get rid of him.

JACK: Well, obviously I'm going to do that, but how can I make sure he goes and how can I make sure he goes without a fuss?

STAN: Have you finished your background check on him?

JACK: Look, what I want to know is, can I just report him?

STAN: Who to?

JACK: I don't know who to—you're the lawyer—tell me who could I report him to!

STAN: Well, yes, there are authorities—You know, you could just call…

JACK: Call?

STAN: You know, those numbers... where people can report their suspicions...

JACK: And I wouldn't have to give my name?

STAN: I'm finding this conversation very uncomfortable, Jack—

JACK: I don't give a rat's arse, Stan—Tell me—And I wouldn't lay myself open to a defamation action?

STAN: Reports of this sort are specifically protected from defamation: you're just doing your patriotic duty, Jack; but, Jesus...

JACK: So I could anonymously report him, and he'd disappear, and that'd be that, right?

STAN: Well, no—it's not that easy—I'm sure there are procedures—

JACK: Then tell me what to do!

STAN: Shit, Jack, are you serious?

JACK: Didn't you hear me? Didn't you hear what I just said?

STAN: Look, I think you need to think carefully about this—I mean, it's a man's career after all.

JACK: I'll do whatever I have to to protect the integrity of this Department.

STAN: The integrity of the Department, Jack?

JACK: Fuck you, Stan, yes; the integrity of the Department; I'll do whatever I have to to protect the integrity of the Department.

Light change.

❖ ❖ ❖ ❖ ❖

SCENE EIGHTEEN

Talbot's home.

TALBOT *rushes in.*

TALBOT: Eve...?

EVE *moves from the shadows.*

EVE: Talbot? Where were you? I was worried.

TALBOT: Eve, something's happened—

EVE: Well, something's happened for me, too—You'll never guess—They bought the movie.

TALBOT: Something's happened, Eve; we've got to go.

EVE: They bought my movie, Talbot—Michael Douglas loves it.

TALBOT: What?

EVE: They're going to pay me six hundred thousand dollars for the option!

TALBOT: For the option, Eve? No. We've got to go.

EVE: Isn't that amazing? Oh, and your publisher rang again—Are you going to call him?

TALBOT: We've got to go, Eve; we've got to get out of here.

EVE: What?

TALBOT: Eve, something's happening.

EVE: What are you talking about, Talbot?

TALBOT: There's this man, Eve; this—person.

EVE: Person, Talbot? What's wrong?

TALBOT: There's this man, Eve; he might be a government agent.

EVE: Government agent, Talbot?

TALBOT: We've got to go, Eve, we've got to get away.

EVE: Why would a government agent be following you?

TALBOT: I don't know why, but he is.

EVE: Talbot; you're not making a lot of sense.

TALBOT: A man is stalking me, Eve; I was attacked in my rooms the other day.

EVE: You said you fell.

TALBOT: I didn't want to worry you—

EVE: Worry me, Talbot?

TALBOT: Eve, please…

EVE: Please what, Talbot? Please abandon everything you've worked for just when it's beginning to pay off? Please what, Talbot? Now we can afford to have a baby!

TALBOT: Oh, no—not now, Eve—no.

EVE: No? No…? What do you mean, no?

TALBOT: Didn't you hear what I just said?

EVE: Didn't you hear what I just said? I have just sold my movie to Michael Douglas!

TALBOT: Who gives a fuck about your fucking movie?!

EVE: What?

TALBOT: Who gives a fuck? When the whole of the United States is hitting the wall; when blacks are being disenfranchised, Supreme Court judges are being bought off, and Presidential elections are being rigged, who gives a fuck if we get one more Michael Douglas movie or not?!

EVE: I...

TALBOT: This stuff you do is shit! Do you honestly expect me to believe that churning out the filthy fucking propaganda you do to make everyone feel all right represents any kind of contribution to human knowledge or happiness?

EVE: I...

TALBOT: Six hundred thousand dollars, Eve? Do you know how much a teacher gets paid?!

EVE: I'm not saying I deserve it, and I'm not saying I'm worth more than you, but I do hope my work makes some kind of contribution to human knowledge and happiness, and I am proud of being a writer! How dare you, you shit!

A slight pause.

TALBOT: All right...

EVE: Fuck you, Talbot...

TALBOT: All right, I'm sorry...

EVE: What am I? Just a propagandist for the machine now? What machine, Talbot? The machine grinding the earth to bits? Aren't we all just little cogs in the machine that's sending us all mad?

TALBOT: A man is stalking me, Eve—a man is hunting me—

EVE: He's not.

TALBOT: He is.

EVE: He's not, Talbot; he's in your head; he's you, your fears, your projections—

TALBOT: He's not! He's real!

EVE *picks up the remote and turns the TV on, channel surfing to show...*

EVE: Where? Where is he? What's going on, Talbot? Are the secret police crawling down the corridors of America? Are there riots in the street? What country are you living in?!

TALBOT: The same country you are, and if you were a black, or a Puerto Rican, or a homeless person on the street, you'd know what country that was.

EVE: This is my country, and I love it; and I'm not saying it's always right and I'm not saying it's always good, but I am saying it is my country and I'm going to fight for it, and fight to make it right, and

I'm not going to run away and leave it to the likes of Don Rumsfeld and Dick Cheney to wreck.

TALBOT: They've already wrecked it, Eve—they wrecked it while we were all asleep!

EVE: I haven't been asleep, and I know that's not true; and I know there was a time when I thought we were happy and you weren't afraid, and I just want to know what happened to that man because I want him back!

TALBOT: What do you want me to do? Just deny what's happening to me? Just pretend that everything's all right! It's not all right, Eve; we are not all right!

EVE: But we're not living in a prison, either, Talbot! This is America!

TALBOT: America has been betrayed! America has betrayed itself! This is not America, this is the lie America tells itself! You want to know what America is, you go to the prisons, you go to the execution cells, you look into the eyes of the men on death row, you'll see what America is!

EVE: I see what America is when I look at you! We are America! This is America! We are making America now! And if it's betrayed, we are the ones betraying it!

TALBOT: No... no... no...

EVE: I want you, Talbot; I want you in my life, but not at any price...

TALBOT: What price, Eve? My life? My sanity? What price?

EVE: I can't order you to love me, Talbot, and if you want to go, then go; but if you go, don't come back; if you go, just go.

A slight pause.

TALBOT: All right...

EVE: You need to get some help, Talbot; I think you're having a breakdown.

TALBOT: Don't use the car, Eve; I've got to get it checked.

EVE: All right? What do you mean, all right?

TALBOT: All right.

Light change.

◆ ◆ ◆ ◆

SCENE NINETEEN

Jack's home.

Lights up on JACK *talking quietly on the phone.*

JACK: Hi—How's it going…?

> AMY *steps into view holding a drink, listening in the shadows behind him.*

Busy? Busy doing what…? Ah-ha… Ah-ha… Well, I've got a couple of hours tomorrow afternoon if you haven't got anything on… That's not what I meant… You know that's not what I meant… How about dropping over, and we'll crack another bottle of Dom Perignon?… All right, sleep tight. Don't let the bed bugs bite…

> *He hangs up.*

AMY: Who was that you were talking to?

JACK: Graham.

AMY: Graham?

JACK: We're going to take the yacht out on the weekend—Stan looked older the other day over at that lecturer's, didn't you think?

AMY: Talbot's?

JACK: Yes, Talbot's. Don't you think he's looking older?

AMY: No.

JACK: No? I did.

AMY: Everyone's getting older.

JACK: It's really an attitude, isn't it? It's about giving up.

AMY: So are you going to give him tenure?

JACK: Who? Talbot? No, I don't think so.

AMY: Why not? Didn't you like his wife?

JACK: It's an attitude, Amy—Most people our age have given up.

AMY: Have they?

JACK: But I haven't given up.

AMY: Haven't you?

JACK: No, there's a lot more I want.

AMY: Do you think I've given up?

JACK: There's a hell of a lot more I want.

> *Light change.*

A security announcement blasts out...

SECURITY: [*voice-over*] This is a Sector Four Alert; would all marshals please report for duty. This is a Sector Four Alert.

◆ ◆ ◆ ◆ ◆

SCENE TWENTY

Jack's office.

JACK *ushers* TALBOT *in.*

JACK: Hello, Talbot, come in—How are you feeling?
TALBOT: Fine.
JACK: Fine? Well, that's good to hear. So there were no—ill effects—from that—incident the other day?
TALBOT: No.
JACK: Well, that's a relief—And you've been to the doctor?
TALBOT: It wasn't necessary—
JACK: Not necessary, ay? Well, that is good news—Do you think that's wise? You need to be careful about these things.
TALBOT: I feel also that I should withdraw my complaint.
JACK: Your complaint?
TALBOT: About the assault.
JACK: Well, we hadn't actually gotten around to formalising—
TALBOT: In that case, I don't wish to proceed.
JACK: You don't wish to proceed?
TALBOT: Given the inability of Security to corroborate my allegation, it seems sensible to drop the matter altogether.
JACK: Well, I must say—Drop it?
TALBOT: Yes.
JACK: Well, that's—um... Good. That's good, Talbot—But only, of course, if that's your considered position—I mean, there's procedures in place—mediators, et cetera—Are you sure that's what you want? You're not feeling pressured to do this, are you? Is anyone bringing pressure on you to drop this complaint?
TALBOT: No.
JACK: Well, good—good—that's certainly—Now—um—now I don't want to appear ungrateful—and, of course, gratitude has nothing to

do with it, does it, Talbot?—either the assault happened, or it didn't, and as you've withdrawn the complaint—of your own free will, as you accede—then the only logical inference is that it didn't take place—

TALBOT: There's no corroborating evidence.

JACK: We-e-ell, it's a fine point, isn't it?—almost philosophical—But as a physicist might say, if you can't see it, it isn't there—So it's got nothing to do with gratitude at all, has it?

TALBOT: What hasn't?

JACK: Well, I'm sorry to say, Talbot, and this really strikes me quite as bizarrely as I'm sure it will strike you, but the reason I called you in is that someone has made a complaint against you.

TALBOT: Me?

JACK: Yes. You. A student has made a complaint about you.

TALBOT: Who?

JACK: Well, of course I'm not allowed to reveal the student's name at this early stage of the procedures—

TALBOT: Margurite Lee?

JACK: I'm not going to tell you, Talbot—Now how formally do you want to approach this? Do you want a staff representative present?

TALBOT: Is it Margurite Lee?

JACK: Let's stick to the point, Talbot.

TALBOT: Did this arise out of that incident the other day? I've put my report in.

JACK: Did you?

TALBOT: Yes, I did.

JACK: The Secretary must have misplaced it—Do you think you could do it again?

TALBOT: But I told you what happened—Yes, yes I do want a staff representative present.

JACK: In that case, you'll need to be formally charged and suspended—

TALBOT: Suspended?

JACK: Of course—we can't have you teaching students with an allegation like this hanging over you.

TALBOT: But it was nothing—She came into my room: I told you what happened.

JACK: So do you want to instigate formal proceedings?

TALBOT: No, I want you to tell me what this is about.

JACK: Do I understand correctly that you are waiving your right to have a staff representative present?

TALBOT: I just want to know what she said.

JACK: Well, if we're clear about the proceedings, the complaint has a number of elements, the first of which is that you are using your lectures to push your own political agenda—

TALBOT: This is absurd.

JACK: I mean, I've seen you in full flight, and you are pretty formidable, Talbot—You debate the students?

TALBOT: I debate, certainly—that's part of my teaching technique—I challenge.

JACK: Challenge? Ah—well, that might be it. You challenge their beliefs?

TALBOT: Well, that's what education is about, isn't it? Challenging beliefs? Presenting new perspectives.

JACK: No.

TALBOT: No?

JACK: Education is about presenting facts.

TALBOT: Facts, Jack?

JACK: Would you call yourself a leftist, Talbot?

TALBOT: What are you talking about?

JACK: You're a leftist, aren't you; you're a liberal.

TALBOT: I'm a teacher.

JACK: But a liberal teacher.

TALBOT: No, I'm a teacher teacher, Jack. It's a Liberal Arts course.

JACK: It's a Politics course, Talbot.

TALBOT: Politics is part of the Liberal Arts.

JACK: Let's move on.

TALBOT: Politics is part of the Liberal Arts—Every university I've ever taught at has taught Politics as part of its Liberal Arts course.

JACK: All right, you've made your point: you're teaching the Liberal Arts in what really is a Politics course.

TALBOT: What?

JACK: Is that why you quoted Marx in a lecture the other day? As part of your Liberal Arts approach?

TALBOT: Marx was a thinker—

JACK: A discredited thinker.

TALBOT: An important thinker. Marx was an important thinker.

JACK: Parsons is an important thinker, Talbot. Rawls is an important thinker. That's why we have them in the course. Fukuyama is an important thinker. Marx is a discredited thinker. We don't teach discredited thinkers in our Department.

TALBOT: Jesus Christ, Jack—

JACK: That's another thing, Talbot: bad language. The student complained, and she isn't the only one—

TALBOT: So it was Margurite.

JACK: The student complained about your frequent and blasphemous cursing and oath taking in class—Is this part of your challenging approach, too?

TALBOT: It's not true.

JACK: It's not true—so you deny the allegation.

TALBOT: Yes—everything! I deny everything!

JACK: Even though all the staff are aware of your mouth—All have heard the way you carry on.

TALBOT: I don't know what you're talking about, Jack.

JACK: This is important, Talbot; blasphemy is important—to take the Lord's name—

TALBOT: Take the Lord's name, Jack? It's a Politics Department, not a seminary!

JACK: And then, of course, there's your history.

TALBOT: What history?

JACK: The previous sex harassment case in Australia...

TALBOT: No! Never! Who said that?

JACK: Do you believe in God, Talbot?

Light change.

◆ ◆ ◆ ◆ ◆

SCENE TWENTY-ONE

Margurite's apartment.

TALBOT *rushes in ahead of* MARGURITE, *who is wearing a red kimono.*

MARGURITE: What are you doing here, Professor? What's wrong?

TALBOT: What's going on, Margurite?

MARGURITE: Going on?

TALBOT: Did you make a complaint against me?

MARGURITE: Complaint?—No.

TALBOT: Well, someone did and they're going to fire me.

MARGURITE: Fire you? How?

TALBOT: They're going to fire me because of what you did the other day.

MARGURITE: What I did? What did I do?

TALBOT: The other day when you came to see me in my rooms.

MARGURITE: That's absurd—Fire you?—Are you mad?

TALBOT: I need to know, Margurite; did you make a complaint against me?

MARGURITE: No—Why would I? I love you, Professor.

TALBOT: Love me?

MARGURITE: Love your work—love what you do—Why would I make a complaint against you? We'll have to organise a petition—organise a strike.

TALBOT: A strike? No—

MARGURITE: They're obviously just trying to get rid of you.

TALBOT: Get rid of me? But why? What did I do?

MARGURITE: Because of what you teach—They're trying to get rid of the leftists in the universities.

TALBOT: But I'm not a leftist—I'm an academic.

MARGURITE: Of course you're a leftist—Don't be mad.

TALBOT: I'm an academic, Margurite.

MARGURITE: But what about your book?

TALBOT: My book?

She holds up a book.

MARGURITE: Your book…

TALBOT: What's that…?

MARGURITE: It's your book, isn't it…?

TALBOT: Where did you get it…?

MARGURITE: I thought you put it in my pigeon-hole after our fight the other day—I thought that was your way of making up.

TALBOT *takes it.*

TALBOT: My book—it's printed—look, it's in print.

MARGURITE: It's beautiful, Professor; it's wonderful, and the way it drives towards its conclusions is fantastic—Of course you're a leftist.

TALBOT: No—no, I'm not a leftist—This is—this is—a study—

MARGURITE: It's more than a study, Professor, it's a diatribe! It's a polemic! You're saying America is fascist!

TALBOT: No—no—no, I'm not saying that.

MARGURITE: Then what?

TALBOT: I'm saying... there are certain... cultural similarities— dangers—yes, dangers—

MARGURITE: You're not saying that at all—you're saying it's happened—you're saying the military-industrial complex is finally sloughing off the remnants of democracy and declaring themselves the rightful inheritors of America—

TALBOT: Where did you get this? Where did you get this book?

MARGURITE: What's going on?

TALBOT: What's going on? Isn't it obvious? I didn't give you this book, Margurite; I've never seen it before.

MARGURITE: Then—who?

TALBOT: There's this man, Margurite—Homeland Security—

MARGURITE: Homeland Security?

TALBOT: He must be—something like that—Homeland Security—Navy Intelligence—How many fucking spy agencies have we got?!

MARGURITE: What are you saying?

TALBOT: Margurite, there's this man after me—someone—The other day I was confronted by an armed man in my room—and I thought— I misunderstood—I named you.

MARGURITE: You named me?

TALBOT: Yes, I named you.

MARGURITE: Named me as what?

TALBOT: Named you as someone I knew.

MARGURITE: You told Homeland Security I was someone you knew? What else did you tell them?

TALBOT: Look, I know what you're thinking, but I didn't say anything.

MARGURITE: What else did you tell them, Professor?

TALBOT: Nothing, Margurite, I didn't tell them anything—But this— [the book] this—why would they give you this?

MARGURITE: Homeland Security gave me this?

TALBOT: Where else would it have come from?

MARGURITE: All right, I think you should go.

TALBOT: I'm sorry, Margurite.

MARGURITE: I'm a Moslem; is that why you named me?

TALBOT: No—I didn't know...

MARGURITE: We don't all get around dressed as rolled-up carpets, Professor—Why did you name me?

TALBOT: I didn't do it purposefully! I thought—

MARGURITE: What?

TALBOT: I thought your father thought that you and I were—

MARGURITE: What?

TALBOT: I thought he might have thought—

MARGURITE: What? That you and I?—Is that what you thought?

TALBOT: Look, Margurite, I was wrong—

MARGURITE: You thought my father thought that you and I were having an affair? Is that what you thought?

TALBOT: Yes—why not?

MARGURITE: Why not, Professor? Because you think I really dig doing it with tired old men?

TALBOT: Stop, Margurite...

MARGURITE: You thought my father thought that you and I were having an affair? How could you think that? You're old enough to be my father!

TALBOT: Well, why else were you there?!

MARGURITE: Why else was I there? How could you say that to me? I was consulting with my professor! Is that what you think whenever someone turns up in your office?

TALBOT: All right, you've told me—

MARGURITE: And that's why you didn't tell me any of this? Because you thought—

TALBOT: I thought I was handling it!

MARGURITE: Handling it, you idiot! You're going to get us both killed!

TALBOT: What do you mean?

MARGURITE: If this is Homeland Security, we are being set up to look like a terrorist cell. I am not a terrorist, Professor.

TALBOT: And neither am I.

MARGURITE: No, you're just a witless academic ashamed of what you've written! Look at it, Professor, this is exactly what you're saying in your book.

TALBOT: It's just not the time.

MARGURITE: What are you talking about? Of course it's the time! Now's the time to say it, while we've still got the time!

TALBOT: I've got to go.

MARGURITE: Where, Professor? Into darkness? Into fear? Look at you: is this the life of the intellect? I don't believe you—Here to accuse me of making a ridiculous complaint when you've done something that could kill us both!

TALBOT: It was a mistake!

MARGURITE: A mistake, Professor? A mistake? How dare you say those things to us in class? How dare you stand and extol—yes, extol—us to be rigorous and relentless in the pursuit of truth. How dare you tell us to be brave. Galileo, you said, Charles Darwin, you said; thinkers who stood for what they believed in, and look at you!

TALBOT: This isn't rhetoric, Margurite, and I don't have a rich father to get me out of it!

MARGURITE: You're pathetic.

TALBOT: No, you're pathetic—What are you?—A middle-class revolutionary who can't wait for the blood to start flowing, but where will you be when it does? I've got a life, Margurite; I want to live.

MARGURITE: Like this?

TALBOT: Tell me what to do!

MARGURITE: What you've told us: think, fight, struggle!

TALBOT: There's got to be another way!

MARGURITE: There are many ways, Professor; Martin Luther King showed a way, Nelson Mandela showed a way—There are ways!

TALBOT: Keep away from me, Margurite, I'm dangerous.

MARGURITE: You're not dangerous, Professor, and I'm not going anywhere; but I want to tell you something before I ask you to leave: I've heard you say how all behaviour is irrational; how no one really knows the reasons they do things, and I've heard you say the same thing is true of individuals and of nations, that everyone lives this kind of dream-life, bumping into one another from moment to moment—

TALBOT: I know what I've said—What's your point?

MARGURITE: My point is I thought a person who could say that must have a special insight; must somehow be able to escape the dream themselves and wake up, but that's not true, is it, because you can't, you're still inside the dream just like everybody else.

TALBOT: This isn't a dream.

MARGURITE: You're not listening to yourself.

TALBOT: This isn't a dream, Margurite—Goodnight.

MARGURITE: Goodnight? Goodnight? There is nothing good about this night, Professor; this is a nightmare.

Light change.

◆ ◆ ◆ ◆ ◆

SCENE TWENTY-TWO

Talbot's home.

TALBOT *is standing in the darkness, hammering on the phone when the other end answers.*

TALBOT: Hello? Barry? It's me, Talbot—Yes, Talbot!—Talbot Finch— You've got my book!... Well, I've been trying to get onto you, too— I left a message— [*He is looking at the book in his hand.*] What's this—?

Wafting through the darkness, we can hear President Bush's 'Axis of Evil' speech playing somewhere in the background...

PRESIDENT BUSH: '... This is a regime that agreed to international inspections—then kicked out the inspectors...'

TALBOT: What? You want to postpone the publication...? [*He's got the book in his hand!*] But I've got...

PRESIDENT BUSH: '... This is a regime that has something to hide from the civilized world...'

TALBOT: What do you mean, you want to postpone publication—?

The sound of a door opening provokes TALBOT *to call...*

Eve? Is that you?

As the television continues...

PRESIDENT BUSH: '... States like these, and their terrorist allies...'

TALBOT: Well, have any copies been printed?

PRESIDENT BUSH: '... constitute an Axis of Evil, arming to threaten the peace of the world...'

TALBOT: No? You haven't printed any copies? There aren't any review copies out there?

PRESIDENT BUSH: '... By seeking weapons of mass destruction, these regimes pose a grave and growing danger...'

TALBOT: What's going on, Barry?

The other end hangs up in his ear, and he demands...

What's going on?!

PRESIDENT BUSH: '... They could provide these arms to terrorists, giving them the means to match their hatred...'

The sound of the shower is heard and TALBOT *lowers the volume with a remote.*

TALBOT: [*to Bush*] Shut up, you moron—Jesus— [*Calling*] Eve, is that you...?

The sound of water splashing onto the floor gets louder.

They stopped my book—Eve? Is that you? Can you hear me?

A voice comes from behind him.

MAN: I don't think she can.

TALBOT *flinches back.*

TALBOT: Oh, Jesus—No!

MAN: She doesn't seem to be about, your wife; where do you think she is?

TALBOT: How did you get in here? How did you get past Security? Stay away from me!

The MAN *picks up the remote and presses rewind.*

MAN: You know, I like this speech, too...

PRESIDENT BUSH: '... By seeking weapons of mass destruction, these regimes pose a grave and growing danger...'

MAN: So President Bush is a moron, is he?

TALBOT: Stand back—I've got a gun.

MAN: No, you haven't.

PRESIDENT BUSH: '... They could provide these arms to terrorists, giving them the means to match their hatred...'

TALBOT: Yes, I have—Stand back, I tell you.

MAN: Sit down or I'll cut your little finger off.

TALBOT: Stop.

MAN: You know I'll do it.

TALBOT: I'll shoot you!

MAN: You haven't got a gun, Talbot; sit down.

> TALBOT *slumps into his chair as Bush continues.*

PRESIDENT BUSH: '... They could attack our allies or attempt to blackmail the United States. In any of these cases, the price of indifference would be catastrophic...'

> *The* MAN *surveys the room.*

MAN: Dicks like you don't believe in guns; though I bet you wished you did now.

TALBOT: So where's my wife?

MAN: I don't know, but I could find out—You know, you've got to sort out this baby thing; it's starting to feel like a real soap.

TALBOT: You've got us bugged—How long have you—?

MAN: Reality, Professor—remember what I told you? Welcome to the real.

TALBOT: What you are doing constitutes a grave infringement of my rights—

MAN: You don't have any rights.

TALBOT: —and makes you and whoever you're conspiring with to deprive me of my rights criminally liable and open to the most severe punishment.

MAN: You should have been a lawyer, but on the other hand you wouldn't have been much good because you actually believe in the law.

TALBOT: Yes, I believe in the law!

MAN: Which part of the law do you believe in, Professor? The part that says the law is blind?

TALBOT: What?

MAN: I mean—hey—if you're not up to it, I'd be happy to give her a little baby-making service.

TALBOT: How could you?—This is my apartment!

MAN: And a very nice apartment it is, too, Professor. It's my apartment.

TALBOT: Who are you? Why are you doing this to me!?

MAN: You're an Arab, aren't you?

TALBOT: What?

MAN: An Arab of the mind.

PRESIDENT BUSH: '... We will work closely with our coalition to deny terrorists and their state sponsors the materials, technology, and expertise to make and deliver weapons of mass destruction. We will develop and deploy effective missile defences to protect America and our allies from sudden attack.' [*Applause.*] 'And all nations should know: America will do what is necessary to ensure our nation's security...'

TALBOT: No, this is too mad—How much do you want? [*He pulls out his cheque book.*] A thousand dollars? Two? How much do you want to leave us alone!

MAN: You poor fucking drip—That's not it: you're mine—That's right, you're mine: your house is mine, your wife is mine, your mother and father are mine—Do you want to watch while I bulldoze their house? How do you think your father'll look having his teeth pulled out—?

TALBOT: This isn't happening...

MAN: I'm going to rape your wife, Talbot—I'm going to rape your wife while you're having your ears cut off in front of me—I'll give her a fucking baby.

TALBOT: Shut up, you cunt! Shut up!

MAN: No, I'm not going to shut up; I'm going to keep drilling into your head till there's nothing but me left in there.

TALBOT: What do you want?!

MAN: What do I want? Let's start with rights. What rights do you think you have?

TALBOT: I'm married to an American woman.

MAN: And what makes you think she's got rights? You know, when people get married to terrorists, things start changing.

TALBOT: I am not a terrorist! Who says I'm a terrorist?!

MAN: I do. In fact, I say you're the worst sort of terrorist of all, the terrorist who hides behind respectability, the terrorist who keeps his hands clean while others go about their filthy business; the terrorist who kills with words.

TALBOT: This is ridiculous—I refuse to participate in this—I have no idea who you are, you have no right to be here—Get out.

The MAN *pulls out his gun and aims it at* TALBOT'*s head.*

MAN: You. Shut. Up. And talk to me about rights.

TALBOT *says nothing. The* MAN *strides across and smashes him across the face with the butt of the gun, sending him flying across the room.*

TALBOT: No...!

Standing over him, the MAN *roars.*

MAN: Don't you understand what I said to you? You belong to me. There's nothing about you I don't know and no one close to you I can't touch. You are an enemy of the American people, and I'm going to kill you.

TALBOT *tries to crawl away.*

TALBOT: No...

MAN: Now talk to me about rights. Talk to me about the rights of those three thousand people you murdered in the World Trade Center. Talk to me about rights and tell me what I want to hear!

Light change.

◆ ◆ ◆ ◆ ◆

SCENE TWENTY-THREE

Jack's apartment.

In the darkness, we hear ding-dong, and then the door opens.

AMY: Oh, Eve...

EVE: Amy—Is Jack in?

AMY: Jack, no—

EVE: Do you know where he is? I've got to see him.

AMY: Jack, Eve?—No—Come in...

Light change.

EVE *anxiously enters.*

EVE: I've got to see him, Amy—Do you know what time he'll be home?

AMY: No—Do you want a drink?

EVE: A drink? No.

AMY *goes to prepare a drink. She already has one.*

AMY: I think you should have a drink—What's wrong?

EVE: I think I'll just go—Could you tell Jack—?

AMY: Sit down and have a drink—What's wrong, Eve?

EVE: Nice place you've got.

AMY: Thanks—Tonic?

EVE: Nice paintings.

AMY: Thanks—Rothko.

EVE: Yes.

AMY: Worth a mint.

EVE: Yes.

AMY *hands* EVE *the drink.*

AMY: Goes with the carpet—Cheers.

EVE: Cheers.

AMY: So what do you want Jack for?

EVE: It's just something—Talbot.

AMY: Talbot?

EVE: Are you here on your own?

AMY: Always on my own: that's the modern condition, isn't it? How old are you?

EVE: Thirty-five.

AMY: Yeah, well, you'll find out; you'll be joining us all down at AA before you know it.

EVE *slugs the drink back.*

EVE: You limbering up for a bender?

AMY: It's the drug of choice, isn't it; Americans love their whiskey. You ever thought of that? Whiskey and witch-hunts: they're what made this country great—You want another?

EVE: No thanks—If you could just tell Jack—

AMY: I'm not expecting Jack home—You see, Jack's having an affair.

EVE: Oh.

AMY: Not that I mind—At least he keeps his filthy hands off me—You sure you don't want another drink?

AMY *goes to refill their glasses.*

EVE: I think I should go, Amy—

AMY: No, come on—a bit of solidarity—pretend I'm part of the sisterhood.

EVE: Sounds like you should be.

AMY: I didn't think you'd let me in—Would you let me in, Eve?

EVE: When did you find out?

AMY: When did I find out what?

EVE: When did you find out he was having an affair? Did he tell you?

> AMY *gives her the glass.*

AMY: No—they never tell you; you've got to discover it yourself. Usually you overhear something or one of your friends rings up—Does Talbot have affairs?

EVE: No.

AMY: You probably just haven't found out yet—Yes, Jack; the great Jack, Jack-off Jack—You know how he got to where he is? He blackmailed the Dean when he found out he had a subscription to a child-porn website—Power's simple when you get down to it, isn't it; but you'd know all about that, wouldn't you; you're communists.

EVE: Is that what Jack said?

AMY: No—I surmised that myself.

EVE: Surmised it, did you?

AMY: Not that I've got anything against communists—You know what the difference between communists and capitalists is? Communists expect us to be angels, but capitalists know we're devils.

EVE: That's witty—Where did you read that? *Laughter is the Best Medicine?*

AMY: So where's Talbot?

EVE: Thanks for the drink—

AMY: Out on the town? Maybe he's off with Jack.

EVE: I don't think so.

AMY: Why? Is there something wrong with him?

EVE: Maybe there is. He loves me.

AMY: Are you sure?

EVE: What's your problem, Amy? Well, I can see what your problem is: you've got a fucked-up personal life and you've got so few friends you're just sitting around here drinking yourself into oblivion hoping you can torture some stranger who might stumble into your lair— you're a real recommendation for life at the top.

AMY: This isn't the top. Life at the top is far worse than this!

EVE: Well, thanks, but I don't have the time.

AMY: Why not?

EVE: Look, if you think I'm going to take pity on you—

AMY: I don't want your pity—your prissy, snooty-nosed pity—Why would I want your pity? Who the hell do you think you are?

EVE *makes a move.*

EVE: Have a good life, Amy.

AMY: Fuck you, bitch—At least I know where my husband is—Where's yours? Up some black cunt's snatch in some crack-house down the Village.

A slight pause.

EVE: You fucking racist turd.

AMY: Well, fucking beg-your-pardon—hit a raw nerve, did I?

EVE: Yeah, you did: the raw nerve of every slimy piece of shit I hate about this country.

AMY: Tell me about it—the crap and the bullshit—Here we are, right? Two white bitches in the richest country in the fucking world, and look at us. In anybody's language, we've got it: we've got the money, we've got the power; fuck, Eve, the scientists are telling us we can live forever if we want, but you tell me one person that wants to live forever; you tell me one person that wants to live another five minutes.

EVE: I want to live another five minutes; I don't know if I want to live forever, but I want to live another five minutes, and maybe another five after that. There's things to do and things to set right, and the sort of shit that's inside your head is one of them.

AMY: Well, have fun, sweetheart: you and all your do-gooder friends can go to hell, because I've had it.

EVE: What have you had? What have you had? What have you ever tried to do?

AMY: You wouldn't know.

EVE: No, I wouldn't—You know, stupid bitches like you living your ridiculous fucking lives telling the rest of us we can go to hell—you go to hell.

AMY: Gee, I thought you and your little social climber husband couldn't wait to hop up on the perch with the rest of us—If you're not here to look for your husband, I guess the only other reason you'd be here would be to suck Jack's dick to get him to give hubby tenure, but you're going to have to wait in line, sister, 'cause there's a lot of other cock-suckers in front of you.

EVE: I'll tell you why I'm here, Amy: I'm here because I'm hoping your husband can help my husband because my husband needs all the help he can get. I'm here because I'm frightened my husband is having a breakdown, because he thinks the Government is after him, and I'm hoping that your husband can talk some sense into him. I'm here because I believe that no matter how bad in other ways your husband might be, that he still has the decency and common humanity to want to help a colleague in need, and if I didn't believe that, maybe I would be someone like you, crying into my whiskey about how fucked it all is without lifting a fucking finger to do anything about it. Maybe I would be someone like you just looking to lay down in my own shit and rub myself around in it for a while, but I'm not, Amy, because I believe in human beings and I believe human beings can change and I believe human beings can find better ways to live. It's not fucked, Amy, you are. You're fucked, and you can go to hell.

AMY: Sorry to disappoint you, darlin', but Jack is the one trying to screw your husband.

EVE: What?

AMY: Oh, didn't you hear? He's got one of his students to make a sexual harassment complaint against him.

EVE: What?

AMY: And guess what—this is the best bit—the student he's got to make the sexual harassment complaint?

EVE: What about her...?

AMY: She's the one Talbot's been screwing.

Light change.

◆ ◆ ◆ ◆

SCENE TWENTY-FOUR

Talbot's home.

EVE *comes rushing nervously in.*

EVE: Talbot...!

TALBOT *is sitting in the shadows.*

TALBOT: Eve...? Where have you been...?

EVE: Talbot, I need to ask you something...

TALBOT: Eve—I don't want you to use the car—you can't use the car.

EVE *sees his bloody face.*

EVE: What's happened?

TALBOT: He was here—he came here—he bashed me.

EVE: Who did?

TALBOT: The man! The one I was telling you about!

EVE: Where? Here? No—How? How did he get in?

TALBOT: He just walked through the door, Eve—He can go anywhere— We've got to get out of here.

EVE: You're making it up—it's not true.

TALBOT: It is true, I tell you? [*Referring to his face*] How did this happen?

EVE: You did it yourself! This doesn't happen, Talbot!

TALBOT: I'm telling you it did!

EVE: I don't believe you!

TALBOT: Then you tell me what's happening!

EVE: Are you having an affair?

TALBOT: What? An affair? What?

EVE: Are you having an affair with one of your students?

TALBOT: One of my students?

EVE: I want to know, Talbot; I want to know the truth!

TALBOT: What truth?

EVE: All this—this trouble—is this because you're having an affair?

TALBOT: No!

EVE: Then what is it, because none of your explanations make any sense!

TALBOT: An affair? Why would I be having an affair? I love you.

EVE: You don't love me, you've used me!

TALBOT: Used you? No!

EVE: You've used me to get yourself into America, you've used me to support you!

TALBOT: No!

EVE: Don't you know anything about yourself at all?!

TALBOT: What?

EVE: Me! Talbot! Me! Look at me! Do you love me, or do you love your own need?!

TALBOT: It's you! I love you!

EVE: Then see me! See me, Talbot! See my fear! And tell me you love me!

TALBOT: I love you! How many different ways do I have to tell you? I love you!

EVE: How could you if you know what I am?!

> *She bursts into tears.*

TALBOT: What you are? What you are?! You're my soul, Eve, everything good in me comes from you; without you I'm nothing. What am I? A head without a body, a mind without a tongue—I don't know what I am, Eve; I'm anger and bile; I'm rage and bitterness; but you make me real, your love makes me real, and I'm sorry for all those terrible things I've said to you, all those hateful things I said, but I just couldn't see a door out of my own impotence; but you're the door, Eve; we can be free.

EVE: Free? How can we be free?

TALBOT: We can be free, Eve; we can be free.

EVE: I love you, Talbot...

> *But then, as if it's all a dream, headlights swing onto* TALBOT, *now lost and alone in the darkness as a voice calls...*

MAN: [*offstage*] Professor...? Talbot tries to run...

TALBOT: No!

> *As another voice calls...*

VOICE: [*offstage*] Get him!

> *Light change.*

◆ ◆ ◆ ◆ ◆

SCENE TWENTY-FIVE PART 1

The Guggenheim.

The four friends approach each other.

STAN: Jack...

JILL: Amy...

> *As a Tour Guide is heard somewhere.*

TOUR GUIDE: [*voice-over*] The Guggenheim collection is one of the largest collections of fine art in the world, boasting works by such wonderful artists as Picasso, Giacometti and Kandinsky and all made available to the public through the generous beneficence of some of the largest corporations in America.

The two couples are being served champagne amidst a shimmering installation of hanging drapes upon which the cornucopia of modern life is being flashed: semi-nude fashion models, Picasso paintings, Israeli Tanks.

STAN: Well, it certainly was a coup having the fund-raiser here at the Guggenheim, Jack...

AMY: Jack just loves coups.

STAN: So I heard, Amy, that you and Jill had quite a time at the Washington Park...

AMY: What?

JACK: Oh, look: there's Sarah Jessica Parker.

JILL: Who's that with her?

JACK: Oh, you naughty thing; you know that's not true—By the way, where'd you get that hat?

Light change.

SCENE TWENTY-SIX PART 1

A cell.

The MAN *appears in a doorway holding electrodes.*

MAN: Welcome to my world, Professor...

TALBOT *is spotlit at the other end of the room.*

TALBOT: What do you want?

MAN: You like quotes, I know you like quotes—Try this one—'If you want a picture of the future...'

As he continues, his voice is warped and distorted into the kind of public announcement we have been hearing throughout the play, blending into the arty installations of...

SCENE TWENTY-FIVE PART 2

The Guggenheim.

MAN: [*voice-over*] '... imagine a boot stamping on a human face—
    forever'.

> *The girls have moved off, leaving the boys to plot.*

STAN: Talbot's disappeared.
JACK: Has he? Good riddance.
STAN: What did you do?
JACK: Nothing.
STAN: Nothing? You didn't do anything?
JACK: No, of course not—And you were right about Australia.
STAN: What?
JACK: That's the reason he had to get out of the place: he had a whole
    string of sexual misconduct cases he'd covered up. From the way I
    hear it, he was lucky not to have been charged with rape.
STAN: Who'd you get to say that?
JACK: It's incredible the kinds of people we're allowing into this country.

> *Light change.*

SCENE TWENTY-SIX PART 2

The cell.

The interrogation begins.

MAN: So tell me, Professor: who was smarter? Socrates or Plato?
TALBOT: What?
MAN: Who was smarter, Professor? Socrates or Plato?
TALBOT: What sort of question is that?
MAN: My question, Professor, and remember, in my world, I get to ask
    the questions: who was smarter, Socrates or Plato?
TALBOT: I don't know.
MAN: Yes, you do.
TALBOT: I don't know, I said.
MAN: Then think!

> *Light change.*

SCENE TWENTY-FIVE PART 3

The Guggenheim.

The tour guide's voice echoes eerily through the halls.

TOUR GUIDE: [*voice-over*]... The world of modern art is the world of shock, surprise and scandal...

> STAN *pulls* JILL *aside.*

STAN: What's going on, Jill?

JILL: What do you mean?

STAN: How come Amy couldn't remember your lunch at the Washington Park?

JILL: She's just drunk—Well, look at what the cat dragged in.

> STAN *sees.*

STAN: Oh, shit...

> EVE *enters.*

> *Light change.*

SCENE TWENTY-SIX PART 3

The cell.

The interrogation continues.

TALBOT: I demand to see a lawyer!

MAN: Well, that's a stupid thing to say, and I suppose it takes a stupid man to say it, so let me put it another way: what was Socrates' question?

TALBOT: He didn't have a question...

MAN: Socrates, Professor! What was Socrates' question?

TALBOT: Stop this... Stop this...

> *The* MAN *applies electrodes.*

> *Aaaagggghhhh!*

MAN: Socrates' question?!

TALBOT: 'What is true?'!

MAN: 'What is true?' See, it's not so hard to do when you apply yourself—'What is true?' And what was Plato's?

TALBOT: What was Plato's what?

The man again applies the electrodes.

Aaaagggghhh!

MAN: What was Plato's question?

TALBOT: 'How do we know what is true?'!

This is echoed in...

SCENE TWENTY-FIVE PART 4

The Guggenheim.

The tour guide's voice continues.

TOUR GUIDE: [*voice-over*] 'How do we know what is true' was the question that finally liberated art from representation...

JACK, AMY *and* JILL *wheel into view.*

JILL: Oh, look, there's the Dean—When are you going to get yourself appointed Dean, Jack?

AMY: Why would he need to do that? He's got everyone running around doing exactly what he wants already, and no one's any the wiser.

STAN *hurries up.*

STAN: Jack...

JACK *looks to see.*

EVE: Jack?

JACK: Eve...? What are you doing here?

EVE: Jack, I beg you; Talbot's gone missing and I don't know what to do.

JACK: Well, he's not here, Eve—

He tries to usher her away.

Why don't we just get out of the way here?

EVE: Jack, I know you know what's going on; he's been arrested, hasn't he?

JACK: Not to my knowledge, Eve, no.

EVE: He was attacked—he was assaulted at the university.

JACK: Attacked at the university, Eve? When?

EVE: Please, Jack, I've gone everywhere—you're my only hope—

JACK: I'm sorry, Eve, I don't have the vaguest idea what you're talking about.

The voice-over continues.

TOUR GUIDE: [*voice-over*] Finally art did not have to be about anything at all; finally art could just be.

SCENE TWENTY-SIX PART 4

The cell.

The interrogation continues.

MAN: 'How do we know what is true?' Good question. It can take you into all sorts of interesting places. How do we know what is true, Professor?

TALBOT: Because we ask, we question, we investigate—

MAN: We know.

TALBOT: No.

MAN: We're told.

TALBOT: No—we test—

MAN: We trust.

TALBOT: Who do we trust? You and your spin doctors?

MAN: We trust authority, and if we don't trust authority, we trust no one—

TALBOT: That's right—trust no one, believe no one, question everything.

MAN: That was your generation, wasn't it?

TALBOT: Yes!

MAN: And it was what Socrates said, too.

TALBOT: Yes, and he was right; and we were right, too, fuck you! And Plato's vision of the Just Republic was nothing more than a call for the dictatorship of the philosopher-king—Is that what you are? The philosopher-king?! Quoting Kafka? Quoting Orwell?

MAN: He is educated.

TALBOT: It was Orwell, wasn't it?—Well, how about this for a quote? 'Power corrupts and absolute power corrupts absolutely.'

MAN: Just not smart.

He again applies the electrodes.

TALBOT: *Aaaagggggghhhhh!*

MAN: Who was smarter, Professor? Socrates or Plato?

TALBOT: Socrates!

MAN: Who's smarter now, Professor? You or me?

SCENE TWENTY-FIVE PART 5

The Guggenheim.

EVE *is confronting the others.*

EVE: You know people, you've got influence, you could ring someone up—you could have him released.

JACK: If I could, I would, Eve, but I'm not sure—

EVE: You can, Jack; I know you can; and I know what people think about you; I know what Amy said—

JACK: What did Amy say?

EVE: But it doesn't matter, Jack; people can change, everyone can change.

JACK: What did Amy say?

EVE: We don't have to be like this—unhappy and alone—we can help one another—I need your help, Jack.

JACK: What did Amy say?

EVE: What do you care what Amy said? What do you fucking care?! You don't love her; she doesn't love you! What do you care?!

JACK: I've got to tell you, Eve; I love my wife dearly, and she loves me; and if you can't conduct yourself with dignity, I'm going to have to ask you to leave.

EVE: Don't you see what you're doing? You're driving us all mad, Jack; everyone's going mad; you can't live inside a lie, Jack; nobody can live inside a lie!

JACK: This isn't a lie, Eve, this is America, and I can live in it quite comfortably.

EVE: They've got my husband! They've got my goddamn husband!

And turning, they look upon...

SCENE TWENTY-SIX PART 5

The cell.

The interrogation is reaching its climax.

TALBOT: Why would you be smarter? Because you're here lording it over me? Is that what makes you smarter?

MAN: No, Professor, that's not what makes me smarter.

TALBOT: And so the person who believes in truth gets to drink the hemlock, and the person who believes in power gets to run the academy. Is that your great insight into human affairs? Well, God, why did we need a special tutorial if that's all it was? Any thug can preach that.

MAN: Because that's not what it is at all, Professor, and if I have to spell it out for you, I will. What makes Plato smarter is that he knew this world was the world of appearances where the truth could never be found, and only a dangerous autocrat like Socrates could deny it, and that's what Socrates was: a member of the privileged elite encouraging the youth of Athens to despise the mob. That's what he was tried and executed for—So who was smarter?

TALBOT: [*floundering*] Plato was no democrat...

MAN: What about you, Professor? Are you a democrat?

TALBOT: Yes—yes, I am.

MAN: Then who's right? You or the American people?

TALBOT: The American people defend my right to freedom of thought.

MAN: There's no such right.

TALBOT: What are you talking about? Of course there is.

MAN: There's no such right.

TALBOT: Speech, then!

MAN: Who's right, Professor? You or the American people?

TALBOT: The American people don't want you doing this to me!

MAN: Yes, they do.

TALBOT: No, they don't.

MAN: Yes, they do, Professor, they do; and they're cheering me as I do it.

The two worlds have now become one, and the crowd of onlookers claps politely the torture performance they've just witnessed while the voice-over fades away...

TOUR GUIDE: [*voice-over*] Our next presentation will be at eight pm. A program of other equally challenging performance pieces can be found at the information desk on the ground floor.

◆ ◆ ◆ ◆ ◆

SCENE TWENTY-SEVEN

The cell.

TALBOT *is sitting forlornly on the cell floor when a familiar voice calls.*

MAX: Talbot...? Talbot...?

TALBOT: Max? Is that you? How did you get in here?

MAX: Geez, mate, lookit you; are you all right?

TALBOT: No; no, I'm not all right, Max—How did you get in here? Is Eve all right?

MAX: Look, mate, you've got to get it together; you've got to stop all this horse-shitting around and get it together.

TALBOT *starts to cry.*

TALBOT: They're going to kill me, Max...

MAX: They're not going to kill you.

TALBOT: They're going to kill me.

MAX: Stop it, Talbot; just stop for a minute: how are they going to kill you?

TALBOT: Just by calling me a terrorist.

MAX: Look, Talbot, you've got to calm down—All this stuff you're saying—it's all in your head—You know that, don't you?—You understand that.

TALBOT: Are you out of your mind?

MAX *decides to change the subject.*

MAX: Hey, lookit this, lookit this I brought you...

TALBOT *sees it's a book.*

TALBOT: What is it?

MAX: It's my book—they brought my book out—Told you it wouldn't take long.

TALBOT: Your book? What book?

MAX: The book I told you about.

TALBOT: You wrote a book?

MAX: Sure—why not? Anyone can write a book.

TALBOT *reads the title.*

TALBOT: *The Hidden Terrorists—The Enemies in Our Midst.*

MAX: Not exactly an academic title, like yours, but it's Jackie Collins' publisher, so I know I'll get good distribution.

TALBOT: You've joined them.

MAX: Don't, Talbot…

TALBOT: You've joined them, that's why you're here—

MAX: Stop it, Talbot, you sound like a jerk.

TALBOT: You've joined them.

MAX: Listen, Talbot, I haven't joined anyone; people have their own ideas, all right? I would have thought you'd be the first to agree with that, and the fact of the matter is, I happen to believe there is a good case for more supervision—

TALBOT: Supervision?

MAX: Look at the risks, for fuck's sake. A fucking terrorist could walk into the subway with an aerosol of sarin and kill a thousand people in fifteen minutes, that's the fucking truth, Talbot; and if you want to countenance that rather than be required to carry a simple ID card, well I think you're in the minority.

TALBOT: That's not what this is about.

MAX: What's it about?

TALBOT: I'll tell you what it's about, Max: the more security we have, the less secure we feel, and one day when they've got the whole joint locked down, and everyone shut up in their own fucking cell, everyone's going to wake up and go, 'Oh, my God, what have we done?'

MAX *takes his book back.*

MAX: Well, I just think you're wrong, Talbot.

TALBOT: Get me out of here.

MAX: You know I can't do that.

TALBOT: Get me out of here, Max, please; they're going to kill me.

MAX: Stop it, Talbot, stop it—No crying, right? You're a man, right? An Aussie—oi-oi-oi—No one's going to kill you.

TALBOT: They're going to kill me, Max, I know they are.

MAX: All they're trying to do is help you, Talbot, that's why you're here.

TALBOT: I'll tell you why I'm here, Max: I'm here because even though I knew exactly what was happening, even though I could plot it step by step, intellectually, I never believed it really; I never believed it really was happening—

MAX: It wasn't.

TALBOT: Because I believed the myth that everything turns out right in the end.

MAX: It does, Talbot, you wait and see.

TALBOT: And even though I could see it with my own eyes, even though my brain could understand it, my heart said no, this isn't happening—

MAX: It's not, Talbot.

TALBOT: But it is; it is, Max, and it's killing us. Can't you see what they're doing? This is the end of the American Republic and the beginning of the American Empire.

　　　Light change.

◆ ◆ ◆ ◆

SCENE TWENTY-EIGHT

A street.

EVE *is standing, handing out leaflets with Talbot's face on them to passers-by who hurry past, spitting at her.*

EVE: Help—Help me—Have you seen this man? Help me!

　　　We can't see his face, but it looks like an Irish priest in full black get-up is moving towards her...

MAN: Excuse me, Missus...

　　　EVE *looks up expectantly, answering...*

EVE: Yes...?

　　　The figure turns, revealing...

MAN: I wonder if you could tell me how to get to the Statue of Liberty?

　　　It's him... Oh, my God, it's him...

EVE: What?

And taking one of her leaflets, he leads her out.
Light change.

◆ ◆ ◆ ◆ ◆

SCENE TWENTY-NINE

Nowhere.

The sound of a heavy door crashing shut sends an ominous thrill through the dark air and TALBOT *is discovered shackled, blind-folded and kneeling beneath an enormous American flag when the* MAN *comes in, still dressed in his cassock.*

TALBOT: No!

MAN: Ah, Professor, you're awake. So good of you to wait up for me— I've got another question for you: who was the last thinker of the Enlightenment?

TALBOT: Stop it, please…

MAN: Come on, that couldn't be a hard question for a smart man like you—We'll answer the question, get your confession over and that'll be that: who was the last thinker of the Enlightenment?

TALBOT: There was no last thinker.

MAN: I'm afraid there was—who was he? If we say the Enlightenment started with Voltaire—would you say Voltaire or Diderot?

TALBOT: No…

MAN: Voltaire, then—'God is a comedian playing to an audience too afraid to laugh'—is that him?

TALBOT: Being able to parrot quotes doesn't mean you can think.

MAN: Try this one, Professor, see if you can pick this one: 'Every man in this room has stood on a pile of bodies, and it is a testimony to the strength of our heritage that we have remained civilized.' Who said that?

TALBOT: You're mad…

MAN: Himmler.

TALBOT: You've all gone mad.

The MAN *takes out the photo of* TALBOT *he took from* EVE.

MAN: Oh, what's this…?

He lets it fall in front of TALBOT, *who starts crying.*

TALBOT: Eve… Eve…

MAN: There, there, I know how you must feel, realising as you do the end of everything you ever dreamt of.

TALBOT: Fuck you…

MAN: Ah, the worm turns…

TALBOT: Fuck you…

MAN: What?

TALBOT: Fuck you!

The MAN *walks across and kicks* TALBOT *over.*

[*Groaning*] Ugggghhhhh…

MAN: You were saying?

Blood is pouring from TALBOT*'s nose.*

TALBOT: I don't care what you do; I know who you are now.

MAN: You do, do you?

TALBOT: You're everything rotten, everything hateful, everything despicable about this system.

MAN: Well, it's a point of view.

TALBOT: You're the fear, the anger, the dumb animal desire to lash out and hurt, the beast.

MAN: I'm the beast, am I?

TALBOT: And what I have to tell you is that we're the same.

MAN: Oh, no we're not.

TALBOT: We're the same; you and I are the same because when I look inside myself, I know everything about you; you are me; you and I are the same.

MAN: Oh, no, Professor, we're not the same. We're not the same because you're going to die.

TALBOT: I know that now, but so will you; so will you die, and this system you're building, this prison will also die; all these things will die because if you are in me, I am in you, and those who come after us will struggle in the same way, struggle with their fear and their hope, struggle with their anger and their love, struggle as all human beings have struggled to find some truth and dignity in this world. You might close this chapter, but you can't close the book.

MAN: And so what, Professor? Is this a declaration of love? If you are in me and I am in you, do you love me?

TALBOT: I love all human beings…
MAN: But do you love me?
TALBOT: Yes.

> The MAN *strikes him hard.*

MAN: Do you love me, Professor?
TALBOT: Yes.

> The MAN *thumps him again.*

MAN: Do you love me?
TALBOT: Yes! Yes, I love you, and feel pity for you, and wish that you didn't feel the terrible fear that's eating out your soul.

> The MAN *stamps down hard on* TALBOT's *hand.*
>
> *Aaaaggggghhhhhhh!*

MAN: Don't bother, I'm used to it…

> *We can hear* TALBOT's *fingers breaking.*

TALBOT: *Aaaagggghhhh!*
MAN: But still, we have unfinished business: who was the last thinker of the Enlightenment, Professor?
TALBOT: I don't know…
MAN: You are. You're the last thinker.
TALBOT: No. Never. There are better people than either of us still waiting to be born.
MAN: What did the Enlightenment stand for, Professor? Tell me.
TALBOT: For hope! For reason!
MAN: For Reason; for Reason, Professor; for rationality.
TALBOT: The future, yes! The future!
MAN: The philosophers looked at the world and thought it was comprehensible and able to be brought within the orbit of human reason.
TALBOT: And it was! We learnt how to feed nations! We learnt how to fight disease!
MAN: And so the great experiment in Reason was begun—Absolute Monarchs were overthrown, the Divine Right of Kings was dismissed.
TALBOT: The slaves were freed!
MAN: Revolutions, Professor, the French Revolution—
TALBOT: The American Revolution—
MAN: Wars of liberation, and then wars of conquest—
TALBOT: No.

MAN: Wars and gulags and concentration camps—

TALBOT: No!

MAN: Till armies prowled the world armed with the means to exterminate whole peoples—

TALBOT: No! That wasn't Reason's fault!

MAN: Until finally we get to Pol Pot's Killing Fields, and where is Reason to go? What is left for Reason to do? Reason has found itself to be nothing more than murderous despair. All Reason leads us to is the Reason to exterminate human life; that is Reason, Professor, so who now would stand as the champion of Reason?

> *Pause. As* TALBOT *begins to speak, the lights come slowly up on* EVE *standing some distance away, watching him. She's not in the room, but she is with him.*

TALBOT: If it is my privilege to be a witness and champion of Reason, then so be it, though the whole world knows how little I deserve such an honour. For while Reason has stood and guided us in the right direction, I have cowardly averted my eyes, pretending not to see what all in their secret hearts know to be true: that we live in a world of brutal injustice dying as we speak in its own stinking poison; that whole nations have been raped, robbed and thrown into slavery so we few can enjoy the pleasures we indulge ourselves with; that for all our pretence at honour, grace and beauty we are broken, crippled monsters plundering the earth; and while Reason points ever clearly the path to justice and survival, I have joined the throng leaping to destruction for fear—For fear of what? For fear of you?! For fear of you mental dwarves with your sticks and your burning crosses and your hate! For fear of you morons quoting literature without understanding it, pawing art without feeling it, breathing air without smelling it; for fear of you and your guns and your madness and your tantrums, for fear of you and what you may do as you were doing it! But Reason still stands unsullied, and Reason will be there in a thousand years time when this new Dark Age will itself be no more than a footnote in history, and on that day, I will have a name, even if it's only the name of victim, but YOU. WILL. HAVE. NO. NAME. AT. ALL!

MAN: You won't have a name, Professor; in fact you don't have a name now—There's just one more thing I want to know. I think I

can see in your book how the myth of Aryan supremacy was
cultivated by the Nazi propagandists and led to the disaster of the
Second World War—I think your argument on that is very clear...

TALBOT: What...?

MAN: But what I want to know is, what's it got to do with us, Professor?

TALBOT: What?

MAN: What disaster do you see the American myth leading to?

TALBOT: If you need to ask that, mate, you haven't been watching.

MAN: All right—time's up—nice knowing you, Professor...

TALBOT: I've got a question for you.

MAN: Too late.

Two other MEN *now move onstage, corralling* TALBOT.

TALBOT: If Faith is to replace Reason, what are we to have Faith in?

MAN: America, Professor, that's enough. That's more than enough.

TALBOT: Fuck you.

MAN: No, fuck you, Professor— [*Calling into the dark*] Show him.

TALBOT: What's going on...?

MAN: 'Know reality for what it is'—Marcus Aurelius, Professor—
remember that?

TALBOT: No—but why?

MAN: Because now we can, Professor.

TALBOT: But why? What danger am I? I'm no danger! You've destroyed
me!

MAN: You're not listening, Professor: because now we can.

TALBOT: Stop! Now you can what?

MAN: Now we can.

As the lights dim on TALBOT, *he retreats to a corner.*

TALBOT: Help! Help! Somebody help me!

MAN: Now we can.

Light change.

◆ ◆ ◆ ◆

SCENE THIRTY

The university.

As the lights come up again, we see MAX *standing at a lecture podium before a collection of dignitaries.*

MAX: ... But in the conflict between barbarism and civilization, a free and open society such as our own will always win, and what these terrible times really represent is the door opening into a bright and secure future.

> *Applause. As he continues, his accent shifts towards an American twang.*

But on a more personal note, I'd like to thank the Faculty—Jack—Professor Tod and the others—for the wonderful opportunity you've given me, and the trust you've shown in inviting me to join the Department. This really is a tremendous responsibility, and one that I gladly take up, for the education of the young is our strongest defence against terror, and I hope you understand that we in Australia are as one with you in this great historical task. Once our young people understand the great cost of the freedoms they enjoy, they have no difficulty in embracing the sacrifices needed to defend them, and we know that, though we trust in our ability to prevail, the struggle against the forces of darkness has only just begun—

> *But from the audience comes a shout...*

EVE: Liar!

> MAX *is only temporarily put off his stride.*

MAX: —But begun it has, and Evil will be vanquished, and the demons of this earth will be defeated and sent to hell—

> *As she makes her way towards the podium, the* SECURITY *guys scramble.*

EVE: Liar!

MAX: —This is a struggle to the death, the struggle at the end of history. Good has triumphed in the past, Good must triumph now, Good will triumph forever.

> EVE *strides up and spits in* MAX's *face.*

EVE: You filthy fucking liar!

SECURITY GUARD 1: [*voice-over*] Get her!

The lights go crazy as search beams criss-cross the stage.

SECURITY GUARD 2: [*voice-over*] Look out! She's getting in the car!

Kerboom!

SECURITY GUARD 1: [*voice-over*] Look out!

Blackout.

The sound of a million sirens going off, and a voice-over is heard.

NEWSREADER: [*voice-over*] '... And in a late development, police report another terrorist car bomb has exploded outside a university function, killing the female bomber. A second woman, a Moslem student, has been apprehended...'

Silence.

THE END

WHAT THE CRITICS SAY...

'*Myth*... is a blast of fresh theatrical air in a cultural and political climate starving for it. Sewell's potent, lucid and elegant play races along like a brilliantly balanced black comedy. But, of course, it's much more than that. [...] Sewell has produced a powerful and robust analysis of the currently conservative politics of the US and a warning to Australia. *Myth* is not a solution to the state of the world. It is a penetrating and beautifully crafted missive to us all.'
Sydney Morning Herald

'A ferocious inferno of fear, defence and enforced conformity.'
The *Guardian* (UK)

'This tough political thriller is no play for the timid. But its violent language and extreme brutality, brilliantly choreographed, are essential elements for an enthralling study of a polarised world turned back-to-front—a Kafkaesque nightmare of state terrorism condoned by liberty lovers in defence of the Land of the Free.'
What's On Magazine

'... its tightly reasoned argument, its relentless stripping away of illusions, and most of all the rage it expresses and the fear it evokes, make it a vintage Stephen Sewell offering ... This is a powerful and timely play.'
The *Age*

'*Myth* is cynical, confronting, devastating theatre that doesn't soften its blows.'
The *Australian*

'a knockout, full of energy, mordant humour, cutting insight ...'
The *Sunday Age*

ALSO BY STEPHEN SEWELL AND AVAILABLE FROM CURRENCY PRESS

The Blind Giant is Dancing
The Blind Giant is Dancing has emerged as a modern Australian classic. Allen, a social economist, is a man of idealist and principled origins and a committed worker for the left—but he has familial poison running in his veins. As his struggle with the leader of his party's dominant right faction drifts helplessly from the political to the personal, Allen becomes increasingly controlled by the cold and unyielding anger passed on to him by his steelworker father. This is distinctive Sewell territory—where individual lives are as equally at the mercy of powerful external forces as they are of scarcely understood drives within.
ISBN 0 86819 492 1

Dust
Interspersed with scenes from a staged historical drama of savage conquest, a tense family drama is played out in a setting of modern desolation. Actor, Doug, is on stage playing warrior leader Avenal who seeks to build a Christian world away from the battlefield. When off stage, he seeks his estranged and distraught daughter, Julie. Fighting mental disorder, Julie seeks security and solace in faith, with the help of her bewildered but devoted husband, Joe. As Sewell draws the audience into this investigation of human nature and the intimate environment of these personal relationships, the edges blur between the theatrical and the real, and the big questions are asked.
ISBN 0 86819 496 4

The Garden of Granddaughters
Max, a world-renowned Australian conductor, returns unexpectedly to Melbourne with his wife, Moriley, for a family reunion. Their

three daughters, Michelle, Fay and Lisa, are in various stages of decline, success and reproduction. Their granddaughters are full of hope, promise and childhood dreams. A loving comedy by one of Australia's most important playwrights.
ISBN 0 86819 346 1

The Sick Room
The Sick Room brings together three generations of a family under one roof to care for the terminally-ill teenager, Kate. As she faces impending death, the other family members find themselves confronting their own lives. In this searing work, Sewell examines the state of the nation and the price we pay for success and affluence. His findings reflect a far from healthy society whose future well-being rests on a knife edge. This is powerful, moving and insightful drama at its very best.
ISBN 0 86819 585 5

Traitors
Set in Russia, ten years after the Bolshevik Revolution, *Traitors* examines, with sustained emotional intensity, the correspondence between cruelty and love, and conflicts of the personal with the political. Against a background of widening inter-factional division at the dawn of Stalinism, the play charts the triumph of paranoia and betrayal over truth and innocence. As totalitarianism begins to grip the body politic, history and political responsibility cut violently across emotional disclosure and personal commitment— in the moral confusion we are forced to question who is betraying whom and to what end. *Traitors* was the first of Stephen Sewell's plays to receive a full professional production.
ISBN 0 86819 413 1

CURRENCY MODERN DRAMA

A collection of significant Australian plays offering critical and historical perspectives on the development of Australian contemporary playwriting. Each volume has a comprehensive introduction written by Katharine Brisbane AM, Hon.D.Litt UNSW, publisher and former theatre critic for the *Australian* (and one of Australia's pre-eminent theatre critics) offering readers an insider's view of the times in which the plays were written. Featuring four or five plays, some previously unpublished and/or long out-of-print, production photos and short biographies of the authors, these collections make ideal course books for the study of Australian drama by a particular period.

Katharine Brisbane (Editor)
PLAYS OF THE 50S: Volume 2
Exploring a new theatre distanced from European realism, these plays mark a journey towards a recognisably Australian rhythmic form and a more poetic, visceral drama characteristic of the theatre later in the century. Includes: *The Multi-Coloured Umbrella* (Barbara Vernon); *The Slaughter of St Teresa's Day* (Peter Kenna); *Image in the Clay* (David Ireland); *The Life of the Party* (Ray Mathew).
ISBN 0 86819 695 9

PLAYS OF THE 60s: Volume 1
This first volume opens the door to Australian contemporary theatre and marks its steady urbanisation. Includes: *The Well* (Jack McKinney); *Burst of Summer* (Oriel Gray); *The Season at Sarsaparilla* (Patrick White); and *The Promised Woman* (Theodore Patrikareas).
0 86819 545 6

PLAYS OF THE 60s: Volume 2
These plays portray a society at the cusp of reform and reflect a deep sense of the need for change. Includes: *Private Yuk Objects* (Alan Hopgood); *The Lucky Streak* (James Searle); *This Old Man Comes*

Rolling Home (Dorothy Hewett); and *Norm and Ahmed* (Alex Buzo).
ISBN 0 86819 550 2

PLAYS OF THE 60s: Volume 3
The plays in this volume reflect the radicalism in public and private life of the tumultuous late 60s. Includes: *A Refined Look at Existence* (Rodney Milgate); *Burke's Company* (Bill Reed); *The Front Room Boys* (Alex Buzo); and *Chicago, Chicago* (John Romeril).
ISBN 0 86819 562 6

PLAYS OF THE 70s: Volume 1
The plays in this volume were landmarks in the development of a rough new all-Australian theatre which celebrated the rude colour of Australian language and mores. Includes: *The Legend of King O'Malley* (Michael Boddy and Bob Ellis); *The Joss Adams Show* (Alma De Groen); *Mrs Thally F* (John Romeril); *A Stretch of the Imagination* (Jack Hibberd); and *The Removalists* (David Williamson).
ISBN 0 86819 548 0

PLAYS OF THE 70s: Volume 2
The years 1973–75 are famously remembered as 'the Whitlam period' and the plays in this volume reveal a new sense of direction. Includes: *A Hard God* (Peter Kenna); *How Does Your Garden Grow* (Jim McNeil); *Coralie Lansdowne Says No* (Alex Buzo); and *The Cake Man* (Robert Merritt).
ISBN 0 86819 552 9

PLAYS OF THE 70s: Volume 3
In this volume covering 1975–1977, the authors take stock of the progress of reform. Includes: *Crossfire* (Jennifer Compton); *The Christian Brothers* (Ron Blair); *A Happy and Holy Occasion* (John O'Donoghue); and *Inner Voices* (Louis Nowra).
   '*The worlds present in these plays have passed away*', says Katharine Brisbane in her introduction, '*but these plays remain a dense and telling record of their times*'.
ISBN 0 86819 599 5

For a full list of our titles, visit our website:

www.currency.com.au

Currency Press
The performing arts publisher
PO Box 2287
Strawberry Hills NSW 2012
Australia
enquiries@currency.com.au
Tel: (02) 9319 5877
Fax: (02) 9319 3649